THE STORY OF SILK

This edition published 2025
by Living Book Press

Copyright © Living Book Press, 2025

ISBN: 978-1-76153-460-7 (hardcover)
          978-1-76153-468-3 (softcover)

First published in 1918.

This edition is based on the The Penn Publishing Company printing by 1918.
All rights reserved. No part of this publication may be reproduced, stored in
a retrieval system, or transmitted in any other form or means – electronic,
mechanical, photocopying, recording or otherwise, without the prior permission
of the copyright owner and the publisher or as provided by Australian law.

A catalogue record for this
book is available from the
National Library of Australia

THE STORY OF SILK

by

SARA WARE BASSETT

PLEASE NOTE

These books were written about 100 years ago and show the way people talked, thought, and acted back then. They tell the story of how resources like cotton, lumber, leather, and gold were developed—a process that depended on the hard work of many people. Sometimes the work was done by those who made the profits, and other times it was done by people who were not free, including enslaved individuals.

We know that some parts of these stories include ideas that we now understand to be hurtful and unfair. Our aim in republishing these books is not to support those old views but to share our history so we can all learn from it. By looking at the past, including its mistakes, we hope to learn important lessons that will help us create a kinder and fairer future.

We invite you to read these stories with an awareness of their time and to think about how far we have come—and how much work there is still to do.

CONTENTS

It Was A Race To Pick The Leaves

CHAPTER I

THE BRETTON FAMILY

adame Antoinette Bretton went for the third time to the door of her tiny cottage and, shading her eyes, looked anxiously up the side of the ice-capped mountain that flanked the garden. There was still no one in sight, and with a shake of her head she returned to the coarse grey socks she was knitting.

It was late afternoon, and through the stillness she could hear the roar of the river, the tinkle of herd-bells, and the faint sound of chimes from the far-away village chapel. How quiet the house seemed without Marie and Pierre! The boy and girl had climbed to the hillside pasture to drive the goats down for milking and Hector, the great St. Bernard dog that had been the children's companion ever since they were born, had gone with them, for Hector was an expert at rounding up a herd. Although he was not a young dog he had the zeal of a puppy; with this he combined the wisdom of a sage, and it was for the latter reason that Madame Bretton never worried about her children when Hector was with them. For to Madame Bretton the boy and the girl were still children. Neither Hector, Marie, nor Pierre had dreamed of being really grown up until the Great War had come and Monsieur Bretton, together with Uncle Jacques, had been called to the colors of France.

Throughout the valley were other boys and girls whose fathers, brothers, and uncles had left their homes behind— boys and girls who were not as old as Marie or Pierre, but who nevertheless were courageously trying to do the work of their elders. Marie was now nearly fifteen, and Pierre was sixteen; but when suddenly called upon to take their father's place, they felt much older. Yesterday they had been children with little to do but play; to-day work was ahead of them, much hard work, which seemed to have aged them in a single night and turned them from boy and girl into responsible grown up persons.

What a different village Bellerivre was with so many of its men away!

Yet how bravely its peasants had responded to the call, and how dauntlessly those left behind had risen to meet the new conditions of living!

"We who remain at home must keep things running in the customary grooves, so that our soldiers may find the town unchanged when they return," had been the cry.

And so these noble-hearted mothers and children had toiled uncomplainingly at garden, vineyard, and loom; had tended flocks of goats and cattle; and had harvested the hay and grain. For Bellerivre, walled in between the river Eisen and the snowy capped Pyrenees, was a fertile valley on which, in spite of the tragedy of national warfare, the sun seemed ever to shine. It was a mere dot of a place, with a vine-covered chapel, a low white convent tucked away among the hills, and a scattering of houses. In the centre of the town stood La Maison de Sainte Genevieve, the home of Monsieur le Curé, the much loved parish priest, who although bent and white-haired was the friend, counselor, and teacher of both young and old. The little schoolhouse where he had been accustomed to meet the children was, however, now closed; for in these troublous war days boys and girls had far more important duties to perform than to learn lessons. There were the great vineyards that striped the hills—these must not perish for want of care; then there were the gardens and hay-fields.

But none of these things, vital as they appeared, were of first importance in the community. It was from quite a different source that the peasants of Bellerivre derived their livelihood—a source peculiar if one was unfamiliar with it, but which had been the primary interest of the valley ever since its people could remember. They raised silkworms!

Not only did the father of Marie and Pierre earn his living thus, but so also did most of the other fathers in that green valley. As long ago as the boy and girl had been old enough to walk they had toddled out into the sunshine and helped gather mulberry leaves; and they had not been much older than this before they had learned exactly what kind of leaves the tiny spinners liked best to eat. The precious grove of white mulberry trees had been planted years before by M. Bretton, and had been cherished with greatest care ever since. Each season new trees had been added and so spaced that their roots might have room to spread. Around each tree a trench was dug to hold the moisture. Some of the trees had been raised from seed and transplanted into the mulberry grove when they were three years old; others had been rooted from slips or cuttings—a much quicker and less troublesome process. It was always necessary to have some new trees at hand that the very young silkworms might have tender leaves to feed upon.

How strange it was that out of the vast variety of vegetation these tiny creatures would eat nothing but mulberry leaves! Over and over again, M. Bretton told his children, people had experimented with the leaves of other plants— with lettuce, spinach, and various of the greens from the garden. But it was useless. The wee spinners scorned every such offering. One woman, it is true, had succeeded in raising a few worms on witch-grass; but they had not prospered, the silk from their cocoons proving poor. Mulberry leaves they craved and mulberry leaves they must have. In time the French peasants as well as the silk raisers of other nations abandoned their experiments and went to learning how to grow mulberry trees, studying with care not only which mulberry was best for their silkworms but also which of the species flourished most successfully in the soil of their particular country.

The more they investigated the more varieties of mulberries came to light. There was the Tartarica, or Tartar mulberry, found on the Volga; the Papyfera, or paper mulberry, from Japan; the Chinese mulberry; and the more common varieties of red, black, and white mulberry. To the soil of southern France the so-called white mulberry tree seemed best adapted, and therefore the French peasants began cultivating it extensively, mingling with it, however, some of the rarer Chinese cuttings when these could be secured.

Many a lesson did the people learn about the mulberry tree while they were perfecting its growth! They found the leaves could be reached much more easily if the top of the tree was clipped so that it would grow low and bushy; this enabled children to harvest the leaves, and did away with expensive labor. But because of the luxuriant climate of France and Italy the trees of those countries could seldom be kept low, and usually gatherers had to use ladders to reach the leaves—a process by which many of them were injured and rendered useless. As no silkworm would touch a bruised leaf much of the crop was wasted. In China, where the trees seldom grew beyond the size of shrubs, the conditions for gathering perfect leaves were ideal; especially as the Chinese cut away much of the under part of the trees, so that the gatherers might go in beneath them. In addition to these interesting facts people discovered that if a single twig was broken from the mulberry tree several new shoots would branch out in its place. This was surely a valuable thing to know. Moreover, they learned that the leaves of the white mulberry were the most tender; that those of the red ranked next; and that the black came last in delicacy. Few French or Italian people used the black, but in the colder countries, where it flourished better than did other kinds, it was used almost entirely. Another delightful discovery of the sericulturists, as silkworm raisers are called, was that when their mulberry trees were once properly planted they would, with good care, live to a marvelous old age—some of them even reaching the dignity of two or three hundred years. But unless snails and other destructive grubs were kept away the trees would not thrive. The finer and more carefully grafted they were the greater the damage resulting from hungry insects. In contrast the wild mulberry with its acid and bitter sap presented far less temptation and therefore lived longer than did the cultivated species.

This and many another lesson did the father of Marie and Pierre have to learn before he could successfully raise mulberry trees—to say nothing of silkworms. He must know how to prepare the mulberry seeds by crushing the fruit, covering the pulp with water, and separating the seeds from the waste part of the berry. He must know, too, how to spread the seeds upon cloth and lay them in the sun to dry, after which they were put away in covered jars, secure from air and moisture, and stored in some dark place until needed for planting.

To Marie and Pierre, brought up amid the environment of many a mulberry grove, these facts were an old story, and how fortunate it was that this was so. Now that their father and Uncle Jacques had gone to the war most of the care of the silkworms would fall to them. There was, to be sure, Josef the old gardener—he could give advice; but he was too old and crippled to do much work.

And therefore it was the two children, together with their mother, who were planning for their first harvest of cocoons, and were eagerly awaiting the unfurling of the mulberry leaves before beginning to hatch out their crop of silkworm eggs. How anxiously they had watched the trees! How eagerly scanned the swelling buds! Ah, it could not be long now. Was not the river a torrent from the melting of the winter's snows? Was not the sun warmer, the heaven bluer, the ground fragrant as if newly awake? Soon the mulberry trees would be sending forth their leaves. Until they did, however, it would be useless to hatch the eggs so carefully laid away, for there would be no food to give the ravenous little spinners should they rouse from their long sleep.

And so Marie, and Pierre, and their mother strove to be patient, contenting themselves in the meantime with preparing the empty rooms of the silk-house, where the caterpillars were to be raised. Many a time they had not only seen this done but had assisted in the process. Every step of the work was familiar. They knew well that the labor of making the place immaculate was far from wasted, for unless the rooms were spotless the fastidious spinners would either sicken and die, or would refuse to fashion their wonderful webs.

M. Bretton, who had spent a good portion of his slender income in constructing the up-to-date shelter that housed his caterpillars, often laughingly declared that their accommodations were far more luxurious than were those where his own family lived. Nevertheless it was money well invested, he argued, since already he had got back from the sale of his cocoons many times over what the plant had cost him. So successful had he been that his example had been followed by many of his more prosperous neighbors until now Bellerivre, tiny as it was, could boast as fine equipment for sericulture as could be found in all France.

Poor M. Bretton! How proud he had been of his handiwork! How modestly exultant over his good fortune! And now that he had been forced to abandon it all and go to the Great War it was unthinkable to his wife and children that they should not take up his work and strive to carry it on. Nay, the very bread they ate depended upon their doing so.

Hence do you marvel that Marie, Pierre, and Madame Bretton labored early and late and denied themselves many things they wanted, that instead the money might be spent to further the industry that M. Bretton had cherished? And since what we work for becomes the centre of our interests it logically followed that all three of them found their task an absorbingly fascinating one. Playtime and study were cast cheerfully aside, and in place of them the boy and girl received each day the more vital compensations that come from unselfishness and hard work.

It was Marie who first detected that the buds near the ends of the mulberry branches were opening.

As she and Pierre drove the flock of goats down the steep mountain trail which led from the plateau where the pasture lay she glanced across the valley. Against the blue sky a tracery of delicate green was showing.

"Pierre!" she cried, "see! The mulberry buds are awaking! Look! Do you not catch that bit of color against the clouds? We will wait no longer. Let us tell Mother to take the silk-worm eggs out of the dark room and put them where it is light. Soon there will be plenty of new leaves. Hurrah, Pierre!"

With a rush Marie bounded past her brother and ran down the narrow path scattering the goats before her in every direction, and sending Hector racing homeward with yelps of delight.

CHAPTER II

THE SILK-HOUSE

arie's prediction proved a true one, for within another fortnight the mulberry buds were tipped with green, and it was evident they would be in leaf with the coming of a few more days of warm sunshine.

"Our silk-growing will begin in earnest now," declared Madame Bretton, "and before it does I think we'd better take one last careful survey of the silk-house to make sure that everything is all right."

From a peg over the fireplace she took down a key, and going out, crossed the lawn to a building which stood opposite. The children danced after her, entering the silent structure with prancing steps. Once inside, however, they stopped their skipping as if automatically and instead began creeping softly about on their tiptoes. Then Pierre glanced up and laughed.

"I declare if we are not as quiet as though the silkworms were here already," said he.

His mother smiled.

"It is force of habit," she answered. "We always have to be so quiet when they are here that it is hard to remember there is no need for the precaution when the building is empty. How odd it is that their hearing should be so acute! No one who has not had the care of silkworms can realize the disastrous results of startling them."

"Father once told me he had known of a lot of silkworms that stopped eating and died because a sudden noise frightened them," observed Pierre.

"Such a calamity is not at all unusual, Pierre," returned his mother. "And more than that, if anything alarms them after they have begun to spin they will frequently snap the thread of their cocoon and refuse to spin any more; if they do continue the interruption causes a lump, or rough place, in the filament so that it is imperfect and has to be broken and tied. In consequence the silk is poorer and brings a lower price. So you see how really important it is not to jar their sensitive nerves."

"Who would think that one of those green caterpillars had any nerves!" ventured Marie. "Is it true, Mother, that a thunder-storm will check their spinning?"

"Yes. It often does if the thunder is very heavy. Your father once lost an entire crop of silkworms because of a severe thunder-storm. The little creatures died of fright. It is wonderful how delicately attuned they are."

"And their sense of smell is so keen," Marie continued thoughtfully. "I remember one day Father hurried me out of the silk-house because I had some perfume on my handkerchief. I was so cross," she added with a shamefaced little flush, "for I thought the perfume very nice and I couldn't understand why he did not like it."

"Miss Vanity!" cried Pierre. "I guess afterward you saw he was dead right. He couldn't take the chance of losing his silkworms, and I don't blame him, either. It is far too much work to raise them; isn't it, Mother?"

"I rather think you will say so when you have raised your own crop," was the quiet answer.

"Do you remember the Italian Father hired to help him once; and how he afterward sent the man away because he would smoke, and smelled of tobacco all the time?"

"Yes. That was another example of the same thing," replied Madame Bretton. "Your father was afraid to risk keeping the man. The caterpillars might scent the tobacco and object to it."

"I had no idea they were so fussy!" gasped Marie. "I do hope our silkworms won't get frightened and die, or else have something make them stop spinning."

"I don't believe they will if we take good care of them," was her mother's soothing answer. "Still, we never can tell. We must heed everything Father has told us if we want to make a success of our task. To begin with there are the mulberry trees—we must not strip them of leaves too early in the season, for if we do the sap will be lost, and the strength of the tree weakened; in addition we must be careful not to waste the leaves by gathering too many at a time, or by getting the wrong kind. You know the worms will eat only freshly gathered leaves. Let us not forget that. And the young silkworms must have small and tender ones. As they grow older they will need more solid food and their development will keep pace with the advancing vegetation. It is the saccharine they take from the leaf that makes them grow; if you feed them tough leaves with little saccharine in them the poor worm has all the labor of eating a vast quantity of material that simply takes its strength and leaves it exhausted and unnourished. Of course we have plenty of leaves to choose from and we shall not need to economize our supply of food. But where people grow silk in great quantities they calculate very closely, and plan to get the greatest number of pounds of silk from the smallest possible number of leaves. That is the way all professional silk-growers work. Paying their leaf-gatherers is quite an expense, and they do not wish this item needlessly large. They buy the leaves by weight, and the leaf purchasers soon become expert in selecting those lots that are the most nutritious; for every one wants his silkworms to grow large and strong so that they may spin fine cocoons and give out a valuable quality of silk."

"Why, Mother, just feeding them is an absolute science in itself then," sighed Pierre in dismay. "I thought if we kept them from going hungry it was all we had to do. We never shall be wise enough to work out such a problem as you have put to us."

"It is not to be expected that we shall," replied his mother kindly. "Such scientific treatment of silkworms takes both knowledge and experience. Many people raise a good crop of cocoons without knowing much more than we do—sometimes not as much. I was only telling you the possibilities of the industry if one were to pursue it on a large scale. If you and Marie and I keep our silkworms alive, clean, and well-fed, and reap a reasonable harvest of cocoons, we must be satisfied. I shall consider we have done well. Only let us not waste more leaves than we must. In time we shall learn to estimate about how many to gather at a picking. Fortunately here in France the mulberry trees yield more leaves than they do in most countries, so I am not worried lest we fall short. In some countries the number of leaves is very limited, and the gatherers are compelled to be exceedingly careful not to waste them. I remember hearing your father say that in Persia, where the climate is very hot, the natives gather small branches of leaves, that they may be fresher than they would be if picked one at a time."

"Why don't we do that here?" inquired Marie. "I should think it would be a fine plan."

"It isn't," responded her mother. "In the first place it injures the trees to take off so many twigs and let so much sap escape; furthermore, it makes more waste to clear away. We should only be making ourselves work were we to follow such a method. The best way is to gather the single leaves just as we always have done. There will be four of us, for old Josef can help us. It is fortunate he did not go to the war, for while he helped your father he learned many things about silk-raising which will be useful to us, I am sure."

"I wish the silkworms did not eat so much," grumbled Marie.

"They must eat if they are to grow, dear," said Madame Bretton. "Every creature eats more while growing—even children," she added mischievously. "But a silkworm does all its growing in a very short space of time, and in proportion to its size grows faster than almost any other living thing. Remember, its whole life is over in a few short weeks. It must live very fast while it lives."

"If only ours *do* live," interpolated Marie dubiously.

"I see no reason to fear they won't," Madame Bretton said

once more. "But we must neglect nothing. It is the trifling carelessnesses that bring bad results—the tiny things that it seems silly to take the trouble to do. If we lose our crop of cocoons because of slighting the little details it will be our own fault, and we shall deserve failure; if, on the other hand, we do the best we know, we shall have no regrets. We must take every precaution to keep the silk-house clean and well-ventilated, for silkworms demand spotless surroundings as well as plenty of fresh air. Then we must not allow withered leaves or other refuse to collect on the shelves where the worms are feeding, for any waste matter ferments and causes disease."

"Aren't silkworms very likely to get sick anyway, Mother?" queried Pierre.

"They are susceptible to certain diseases," nodded Madame Bretton. "For example, there are epidemics which sometimes sweep away the hatching of an entire season; sometimes, too, the eggs are diseased and hatch into diseased caterpillars, which in turn lay more diseased eggs. This was the tragedy that befell France in 1847. At that time the French people could get no healthy eggs anywhere in their own country, and were forced to send to Italy for them. Afterward the infection spread to Italy. Then those from the region of the Danube, where growers had been purchasing them, also became diseased. The plague spread even to China, until in 1865 the only good eggs to be had were those from India. You can imagine what a terrible experience that was for the peasants. Not only did they lose all the eggs that they had raised and stored, but as most of them were poor they could not afford to import perfect eggs from India. Hence many of them gave up silk-raising entirely and the price both of silkworms and of silk became enormous. Only the very rich could afford to buy either."

"How did people ever get out of such a tangle, Mother?" questioned Marie, much interested.

"Little by little those fortunate persons who secured good eggs sold a few to those who had none, and the crop soon increased, for one silkworm-moth will lay as many as two or three hundred eggs. But even at this rate it took many years to get the industry up to where it was before. It was a terrible misfortune to the French and Italian peasants, and you may be pretty sure that as a result of the calamity every one set about being careful to prevent another such disaster. Now when silkworms are ill they are quickly isolated, just as people are who have contagious diseases. And if there is danger of wide-spread infection, and the growers think best not to take any risks, they will even kill many of the caterpillars outright. The sacrifice is sometimes great, but it is a necessary precaution. Furthermore, present day sericulturists have learned much about growing silkworms, and the importance of keeping the silk-houses clean and well aired; they have found that they must preserve an even temperature within the buildings; wash the walls down with lime to purify the atmosphere; sterilize the trays from which the worms feed; and hatch the eggs in large, airy places. The most up-to-date growers who work on a large scale use incubators. Of course, however, there are still some ignorant peasants who insist on hatching the caterpillars inside their clothing, where the warmth from their bodies will bring the eggs quickly to maturity. Fortunately there are not many who do this. They have learned better."

"I should hope so!" ejaculated both Marie and Pierre in a breath.

There was a moment of silence; then the boy looked up into his mother's face and said:

"I understand now why Father was so particular."

"Your father is an intelligent man, who believes that 'trifles make perfection and that perfection is no trifle,'" answered Madame Bretton. "He has raised some very fine silk and made a good profit by selling it. But every franc of the money was earned—it never came to him easily."

"We'll try to do as well as he has, won't we, Mother?" Marie said softly.

"We must not expect to do anything as well as your father would have done it; he has been a very successful silk-grower. But we will do as well as we are able," returned Madame Bretton with a sad, far-away glance.

CHAPTER III
PÈRE BENEDICT

hen Madame Bretton and the children returned from their inspection of the silk-house they were surprised to find Monsieur le Curé, good Father Benedict, awaiting them. The priest was sitting contentedly in the sunshine, his walking-stick in his hand, and the gentle breeze stirring his white hair. Beside him stood Hector with nose on the Curé's knee and great brown eyes looking into the kindly face of the old man.

Madame Bretton hurried forward.

"Why, Father!" she exclaimed. "Who would have thought of finding you here! Have you been waiting long?"

"But a few minutes, my dear," was the answer. "I knew well you could not have strayed far, for the house was unlocked, and the kettle steaming on the hob."

"So it was," laughed Madame Bretton. "You must stay and share our porridge with us, Father. It is just supper time, and you have had a long walk from the village. You must be hungry. The children and I would be so glad if you would be our guest."

Marie and Pierre added their pleas.

"Do stay, Father," they cried. "Stay and tell us some stories."

Monsieur le Curé smiled into their eager faces.

"I will gladly stay if you are sure the porridge——"

"There is enough, Father, and to spare," declared Madame Bretton. "But had I known you were coming you should have had one of the hot tea cakes that you like so much."

"Ah, a tea cake—how good it is! You are a rare cook, my daughter." He glanced into Madame Bretton's face with radiant smile. "But is not hearty welcome better than a pyramid of tea cakes? If you are sure about the porridge——"

He chuckled playfully.

"There is plenty, Father—plenty," put in Marie. "I saw Mother measure it. And if there weren't you should have mine," she added as she joyously seized his baretta and stick and hurried away with them.

"You are a good child, Marie," the old priest called after her. "Now make haste to put my things away, and then you and Pierre shall come here and tell me how your silk-raising is getting on. Have you begun to hatch out your silkworms yet?"

The boy and girl nestled at his side. Had not Father Benedict brought them up; and was he not friend as well as teacher? In every home in Bellerivre his coming was hailed with delight, and his departure followed with regret. He possessed the rare attributes of sympathy and simplicity sometimes blended in great natures. None of his flock experienced a happiness too trivial for him to exult in, or a grief too personal for him to share.

Madame Bretton glanced for a second at the group on the door-step—at the white-haired man, the bright-faced children, the old dog; then she softly tiptoed into the house to make ready the evening meal.

"We haven't hatched any of our silkworms yet, Father," answered Marie, "but everything is prepared, and we shall begin in a day or two; perhaps to-morrow if there is warm sun."

"That is right," nodded the priest. "It is full time they were under way. That is one reason I came to see you. You live so far away that I feared you might not know that all through the valley the silk-raising is beginning. Already some of the peasants in the village have hatched their eggs; but I think they were a bit too hurried about it, for the trees are hardly leaved out enough yet. Sometimes it is as bad to be too early as too late. I hope you are going to have fine luck, my dears, fine luck! And indeed I don't see why you shouldn't."

"We hope so too, Father. It means a great deal to us to succeed, you know," responded Pierre gravely. "You see it is not alone that we need the money for ourselves. It is for Mother as well; and so that we may also send things to Father and Uncle Jacques."

The priest patted the boy's head.

"I know, I know," he answered softly. "Well, be of good courage, my children, and do not be disheartened if you meet with failure at the start. Try a second time, and a third, and many more. The people who first raised silkworms had to try and fail many, many times before they succeeded."

"Who did first raise silkworms, Father?" questioned Marie. "I was wondering about it the other day. Where did we get the first silkworm eggs, and who thought of reeling the silk from the cocoons?"

"That is a pretty big question, Marie," laughed Father Benedict. "Nobody can be exactly sure who originated the industry of sericulture. Certain it was, however, that before other countries had sugar, or china, or silk, the Chinese people were producing all of these things. But they were a selfish nation, and jealous of allowing any one else to share in their progress. Therefore they shut the rest of the world out of their discoveries and kept to themselves the secret of how they obtained the products they manufactured. For China, you must know, was a great walled country where travelers were not very welcome, and whose people mingled little with the inhabitants of other lands. How the Chinese learned to make silk we do not know; but there are in existence old records showing that as far back as the year 2700 B. C., these ingenious people were making fabrics spun from the filament taken from the cocoons of the silkworm. There is an ancient story that the Empress See-ling-shee hatched and raised silkworms in her garden, afterward winding the silken thread from the cocoons and weaving a delicate gauzy tissue from the fibres. Who taught her to do it no one can tell. Some persons think the Chinese stole the art from India; certain it was that the inhabitants of Persia, Tyre, and other eastern countries got silk thread from somewhere at a very early date and used it. In fact it was because the Greeks and Romans called the land beyond the Ganges 'Seres' that later the name sericulture became the term applied to silk-raising."

The priest paused and gently stroked Hector's head.

"There are many ancient references to the use of silk," he

went on. "We read how Alexander the Great brought home from Persia wonderful silk fabrics when he and Aristotle went there to collect curiosities. He even tells how the silkworms produced this material which, by the way, he calls bombykia; but nowhere does he tell in what place the industry had its origin. However, he at least knew more about it than did most people, for the common opinion was that the tissue was made from wool, or the fibre of trees, some persons even thinking it came from the bark. Another notion was that silk was woven from thread spun by the spider; still others argued that the cocoanut was its source."

"How stupid of them!" ejaculated Marie.

"Ah, it was not really so strange after all, my dear," replied the priest. "Suppose you were seeing silk for the first time. Where should you think it came from?"

"I don't know."

"Precisely. And that is just the way the rest of the world felt at that time," continued Père Benedict. "Nobody knew, and in consequence everybody made the best guess he could. Until the time of Justinian, silk-making was confined wholly to China, being in fact little known anywhere in Europe before the reign of Emperor Augustus. What little silk there was cost so much that no one dreamed of wearing it. At last, however, some of the women of the royal houses of Rome ventured to use it for robes of state; and then the very rich men gradually followed their example and began to use it a little, for it was a cool, light material to wear in hot weather. Weavers had not learned at that time to make the rich silks such as we have to-day; nor were the heavy kinds considered so beautiful as were the thinner varieties. But in time it became the common opinion that such fragile textiles were no material for men to wear; the Emperor feared the custom would make them vain and foppish. Accordingly a law was passed forbidding male citizens to use silk apparel."

Pierre laughed.

"But the Romans were no longer content with their coarse woolen robes," went on Monsieur le Curé. "They had seen silk and they wanted it. They were a luxury loving people who eagerly caught up every form of elegance that came in their way. Many of the rich had enjoyed the splendor and comfort of silken garments and they were not to be deterred from possessing them. Persian traders who possibly got their silk thread from China, and who held the monopoly of the woven fabrics, began sending their goods to Rome, charging for them most outrageous prices. Then came the Persian invasion, and the program was reversed; for Rome turned on the Orientals, levying such a high tax on the manufacture of silk that the industry of the Persians was greatly injured. And all this time that the Romans were wearing silk and fighting about it they were still unable to find out where the silk fibre came from."

Père Benedict broke into a hearty laugh.

"Did they ever find out?" inquired Marie whose eyes had scarcely left the face of the priest.

"Of course they did, silly!" was Pierre's scornful response.

"Gently, son, to your little sister," said Monsieur le Curé.

Pierre flushed.

"They did find out, Marie," continued Père Benedict kindly. "And it was in a strange way, too."

"Tell us!" exclaimed both the boy and girl simultaneously.

"It chanced that there were two monks who were sent on a mission to India, and who ventured within the borders of China. While there they saw the Chinese raising silkworms, and returning to Rome they related their story to the Emperor Justinian."

"I think it was mean of them!" announced Marie with spirit.

"I'm afraid it was, my child," agreed Father Benedict. "Yet after all was it quite fair for the Chinese to keep to themselves a thing which it was for the world's good to know? Was not such a course both narrow and selfish?"

"Perhaps it was."

"Well, at any rate, the monks were sent back to China with orders to procure some of the silkworm's eggs. Now this was not an easy task, because no one was allowed to carry such treasures out of China. Had a traveler been discovered doing so he would certainly have been killed. Hence the problem was how to accomplish the feat."

Marie and Pierre edged closer.

"The story goes that the wily monks had some hollow staffs made, and that inside these they stowed away the precious eggs, departing out of China in the guise of pilgrims. On their arrival in Rome the eggs were hatched and the stolen silkworms became the ancestors of all the silkworms in Europe—perhaps the great-great-great-great-grandparents of the very ones you are going to raise next week."

The boy and girl laughed merrily.

"The rest of the story is that Emperor Justinian had mulberry trees planted throughout the Roman Empire and brought to Rome weavers from Tyre and Berytus. These

"IT IS LIKE A FAIRY STORY"

workmen trained other weavers, and in the meantime more and more eggs were hatched. All Europe seized upon the industry. Mulberry trees were planted in Greece and in other countries where the climate was sufficiently warm to make them grow. From Greece the trade spread at a later date to Venice, at that time one of the foremost patrons of the arts. But all the silks made up to this period were very plain, because it was not until long afterward that manufacturers learned how to make velvets, satins, and brocades. Then came a revolution in China, and for the next six hundred years Rome and Greece had the principal supply of silkworms and the monopoly of the industry. Was it not fortunate now, Marie, that the Romans had stolen the secret of making silk?" Père Benedict pinched her cheek playfully. "Had they not done so the art might, perhaps, have been lost, as were so many other of the early arts. Numberless other conquests and wars in various countries followed. I won't stop to tell you about them; but one of the good results evolving out of the turmoil was that silk-making spread to Sicily, Italy, and Spain."

"And France—was she left out, Father?" asked Pierre anxiously.

"Have no fears for your native land, my son. France came into her silk-making heritage about the time of Francis I. England followed her example more slowly because, you know, our English brothers are a little more conservative than we are. All in good time, however, England made silks and very beautiful ones, too, in which her kings and queens were resplendent on state occasions."

"It is like a fairy story, Father," murmured Marie.

"Then you are not tired?"

"Tired!"

The priest smiled.

"At the beginning of the sixteenth century Bologna had the finest throwing mills for the twisting and spinning of thread then known. But China with its peculiarly fertile soil still continued to be the land best adapted for raising raw silk, although several other countries surpassed it in the manufacture of fabrics. In Italy silk-making like glass-making was held to be one of the most honorable of occupations; and silk-makers intermarried with the nobility, being accorded equality of rank with the best born families."

Père Benedict paused for breath; then gave an odd little chuckle.

"I could tell you many an amusing tale of the early uses of silk," he said. "Picture, for example, Henry V celebrating his victory at Agincourt by putting purple silk sails on his ships! And think of Queen Elizabeth receiving as a gift a pair of knitted silk stockings which, by the way, so spoiled her for wearing woolen ones that she disliked ever to wear them again. Silken hose were a rarity in those days, even for queens. Now of course as people saw more and more uses to which silk could be put they came to want it; and the monarchs of all countries, realizing that silk-making would bring money into their coffers, urged their subjects to take up sericulture. Henry IV of France did much to make it popular among the French peasants, offering rewards to those who would grow mulberry trees. England was found to have too cold a climate for silk cultivation; so James I, who was king at that time, tried to have the industry transplanted to the new colony of Virginia. This plan did not succeed, however, as the American planters found the growing of potatoes and tobacco far more profitable. In 1732 another attempt was made in the American states of Georgia and South Carolina and was again abandoned, because although America could raise both mulberry trees and silkworms she lacked the supply of cheap coolie labor in which the Orient abounded. Now the producing of raw silk is left to China, Bengal, the Coromandel coast, India, France, Italy, and Turkey. Bengal proves an ideal silk-raising country, for because of the climate there are yearly three crops of cocoons—one in March, one in July, and one in November. Some of the other countries have two crops; others only one."

"And France?" put in Pierre.

"Ah, Pierre, there should be no need for me to tell you, a French boy, of your own land. The growing of our silk, as you know, is done in our southern provinces; while its manufacture takes place in our great northern cities. Marseilles is the big market for raw silk, and Lyons the centre for the manufactured fabric. Meanwhile England has come to excel in silk manufacture and she now excludes our French made goods whenever she can that her people may patronize their own makers, who get their silk from the English colonies. And it is in this great and wonderful story of silk-making that you and Marie are now to have a share," concluded Father Benedict. "May you and your good mother be successful in a work that has brought to our beloved France much of her prosperity."

There was a moment of silence.

Then Madame Bretton came to the door.

"Supper is ready, Father, and I beg you come in quickly—for while you have been talking I have made you a tea cake!"

The venerable priest smiled with pleasure, and with a child clinging to each of his hands he passed into the tiny cottage.

CHAPTER IV

A SUPPER PARTY

he interior of the Bretton home was extremely simple; and simple, too, was the supper laid out upon the sand-scoured table. In war time even the more well-to-do families were living on the plainest of rations, that all the food which could possibly be spared should be sent to the men on the fighting lines. There was no sugar, little salt, a scant quantity of flour, and no meat to be had in the village. Still no one complained. Was not each serving his country by denying himself those things which, after all, could easily be done without? Healthy boys and girls were as well off—nay, better—without cakes and candies, the grown-ups said; and even the children themselves had come to admit this.

Therefore the little group ate without comment their frugal meal, thankful that their food was as plenty as it was. The kind old priest, like his people, was accustomed to scanty fare, and would have been the first to reprimand his parish-ioners had any of them offered him anything else. Simple, however, as was the supper it was well-cooked and satisfying; and after the chairs had been pushed back, and Marie and her mother had washed the few dishes, a candle was lighted and the Brettons, together with their guest, drew their seats into the circle of its radiance.

"I wish, Father, you would tell us how they make velvet," ventured Marie, who delighted in the Curé's stories. "That, too, is made from silk, isn't it?"

"Velvet!" ejaculated the priest. "What a frivolous little damsel you are! Are you planning already how you will one day dress yourself in the clothes of a princess, my dear?"

Mischievously he pinched her cheek.

Marie laughed.

"No, indeed, Father. It was only that on Sunday when I saw the hangings about the high altar it came to me of a sudden to wonder how the velvet was made."

"You would much better have been thinking of your prayers, naughty one," replied Père Benedict, touching her hair lightly with his long, slender fingers. "However, in order that you may not a second time fill your mind with such questions I will tell you what I can about velvet making."

With a sigh of pleasure Marie settled back onto the tiny stool at the priest's feet.

They all loved to listen to the Father's tales.

"He is better than any story-book!" Pierre often declared.

"The first velvet we know anything about," began the Curé, "was probably brought from India, where it must have been woven on hand-looms. When the Greeks and Romans invaded the East, among other spoils they brought back with them great webs of crimson velvet, with which they immediately began to decorate their palaces. They had no idea how it was made, and of course did not give it the name it now bears. Instead they called it *Villosus,* meaning *shaggy hair.* It is from this quaint old term that our modern word velvet is derived."

The children smiled.

"It was not strange they should have chosen that name, for you must remember they had never seen woven material with a fur-like pile, or nap, such as velvet has; and it must have puzzled them not a little. So you see it is due to these conquests of the Orient that velvet found its way into the world. As time went on the supply of velvet increased. People in other places than India learned to make it. By the fourteenth century it was extensively used for hangings in the churches of France and Italy, and was also much seen at court. Robes of blue velvet marvelously embroidered in gold, which evidently had been worn by church dignitaries, have been found in an old French church, and are carefully preserved as curiosities, since all the velvet of that period was either black or of a crimson color. Now as lace-making was one of the arts of the time, and as much wonderful hand-made lace was used on vestments and altar-cloths, you can readily understand how velvet was a rare means of showing it off, and became a favorite material for church use."

He paused thoughtfully.

"And not only did it rise in favor in the churches, but also kings, queens, and noblemen purchased all of it they could afford, to adorn themselves. It was far more expensive than silk, which at that early date was very costly. In fact it is only since present day manufacture has mastered the art of making velvet less expensively that its price has lessened. Although some of the rare patterns and some of the silkiest qualities are still made on hand-looms, the greater part of it is now made by machinery. The coronation robes for the King and Queen of England, for example, are always made on hand-looms."

"Is velvet hard to make, Father?" inquired Pierre.

"Yes. Good velvet weavers are few. You see when our king Louis XIV of France drove the Huguenots, who were famous silk and velvet weavers, out of the country, they took with them the trades of silk and velvet making. Some carried the art to England; some to Germany. The German towns of Elberfeld and Krefeld now make a large part of the velvet used by the world—or did before the war. Krefeld alone has one hundred and twenty velvet factories, besides many others devoted to dyeing the silk from which the velvet is made. The German Government gives to those who will follow the industry free instruction in the chemistry of dyes, in designing, and in other branches furthering the manufacture. As a consequence the making of velvet has increased there until now many varieties formerly only obtainable in other countries are now woven in Germany."

"But some of our own French cities make velvet, too, Father," protested Marie.

"Ah, surely, dear child! The velvet from Lyons has long been famous. Lyons and Genoa, many persons say, make the most beautiful velvets there are to be had. Some are of exquisite design, having great flowers, scrolls, or garlands brocaded upon them; others are of solid color—a rare and rich shade—and are made from the purest of silk, which gives to them a sheen wondrous to see. Such velvets are, of course, very costly, and only the rich can afford them; but as a product they are a magnificent achievement. You see velvet-making has now become a well-perfected art. Time has eliminated ancient methods, and bettered machinery so that effects never before dreamed of can now be obtained. There is, for example, the soft panne velvet made by pressing the goods after it has been woven until it presents a satiny finish, then there is what is known as mirror velvet, a product woven from more than one shade of silk, and which in a strong light has a changeable quality."

"It is wonderful, isn't it?" murmured Madame Bretton, who was leaning forward and listening as intently as were her boy and girl.

"Yes; all that man thinks out with his brain and perfects with his hands is wonderful," agreed the priest. "It is a test of ingenuity and patience, and as such should be respected. Moreover, velvet is a useful product. The best silk varieties are very durable. They ravel little, and can be steamed almost to their original freshness when they become worn. Of course cheap velvets and plushes—which are merely velvets with a longer nap—are another matter. There is much cotton in them, and consequently they catch the dirt, and are soon defaced. More and more they are passing out of use as coverings for furniture, or for seats in cars and halls. The material cannot be cleaned, and as a collector of dust is most unhygienic. It is well it should give place to something that is not such a fosterer of germs."

"Won't you tell us how they make the fur on the velvet, Father?" begged Marie, who was fearing every moment that the good priest would insist on starting homeward.

The Curé laughed.

"You'll have me here until midnight, little one," said he. "Should I tell you just how velvet is made it would take me hours; nor, in fact, am I sure I know every step of the process. I do know, however, that the soft nap is made by drawing the threads of the silk warp over an extra wire which leaves millions of tiny loops standing upright, and packed very close together all over it. In order that the velvet may be smooth, these loops must be perfectly even and very near together. The closer they are, the more rich and beautiful will be the velvet. It is when these loops are cut that we get the silky sheen of the goods. If they are not cut we have instead the material known as uncut velvet, largely used for upholstery purposes. Yet another variety called raised velvet is made by having loops of different lengths so arranged as to form a pattern. Sometimes, too, we see figures of velvet woven into backgrounds of satin. I am sure I need not tell you the name for that sort of goods."

"Brocade!" Marie cried.

"Quite right!" nodded the priest.

"And velveteen, like my trousers, Father—what about that?" questioned Pierre.

"Velveteen? Velveteen, my boy, was first made in England, and is a less expensive material, made largely of cotton."

Pierre looked disappointed.

"Nay, nay, son," exclaimed the kindly priest, noticing his face, "do not scowl at your clothing. Velveteen is a warm and durable kind of cloth, and is most useful. Only a prince would be raising silkworms arrayed in a costume of real velvet; and even then, were he to do it, he would be an extravagant fellow."

"Is velvet made in America?" Madame Bretton asked.

"America makes almost no velvet cloth, but much velvet

ribbon, some of which is very fine. The American mills also turn out a great deal of cheaper, cotton-backed velvet ribbon. The best quality of their silk velvet variety is made on looms the exact width of the goods, and has a selvage and back of satin."

"Can people make——" began Pierre.

But the priest had sprung resolutely to his feet, and was standing with his fingers pressed to his ears.

"No more! No more!" he cried. "Not another question will I answer. See, it is already past your bedtime. Besides, I myself must be getting home. Would you keep me here forever? Run fetch my hat and stick—off with you!"

They flew to do his bidding.

Then with a good-night kiss on the brow of each child, and a wave of his hand to their mother, he was gone.

CHAPTER V

THE SILKWORMS

The next few weeks were such busy and exciting ones for the Bretton family that not only did Marie and Pierre find no time for play but Madame Bretton herself could scarcely snatch the necessary moments to cook the meals. Josef, the old servant who had always helped Monsieur Bretton about the silk-house, and who had been too feeble to go to the war, started low fires in the building where the eggs were to be hatched and kept the great rooms at an even temperature in readiness for their coming occupants. The eggs when exposed to the air were so small it seemed incredible that out of them could come the hungry little caterpillars who would spin that delicate silken filament.

"They are about the size of mustard seed, aren't they, Mother?" remarked Marie.

"Just about, and they also are not unlike mustard in color," replied her mother, "although they will not remain so—at least we hope not."

"Why?"

"Because after three or four days they should turn to a light slate color if they are the sort of eggs we want. Those that remain yellow are the unfertilized ones and will be of no use to us; we must discard them."

"And do the eggs always remain slate color until hatched?" questioned Pierre.

"No, they next turn to a dull, brownish slate tint and then the caterpillar comes out. The changes may take place more rapidly than this and the entire process require but a day or two. It all depends on the temperature and the light. Josef knows by long experience just what to do to hurry things along."

As Marie and Pierre glanced at the immaculate white shelves that awaited the newcomers, and realized that for the first time the actual care of the work they had so many times idly watched was upon their young shoulders, it seemed like a dream.

"Now there are many pitfalls which we must be careful to avoid," announced Josef. "In the first place we must beware of rats, mice, spiders, ants—even chickens. All of these creatures can work havoc among the caterpillars. Probably you will not need to worry about them very much; certainly not the rats, mice or chickens. Hens and chickens cannot get in here if you are watchful and close the doors. As for the rats and mice, your father has pretty thoroughly exterminated them. Spiders and ants will find little encouragement in a clean place like this, but we must be on the lookout for them, because one never knows when they will creep into a building. The greatest danger, aside from some epidemic spreading and destroying your crop, lies in feeding your silkworms wrongly. Remember, they must have no wet leaves if we want them to live. You know that already, I guess, or you ought to, for you certainly have gathered enough food for them. Moist leaves will make silkworms ill sooner than almost anything else. So never get leaves that are wet with dew or those that have been rained on. When it looks as if a storm was coming pick a sufficient number of leaves in advance and keep them fresh and cool in the cellar."

"The picking does not trouble us so much as the feeding, Josef. We have never done that. How many times must we feed the worms?"

"At the beginning three times a day; and never forget that the young worms must have the youngest and most tender leaves. Later they will need the tougher ones, with more solid food elements in them, but not at first."

"They are pretty fussy, aren't they, Josef?" laughed Marie. "Lots more particular about their food than we are. Mother makes us eat what is set before us, and never allows us to argue as to whether we like it or not; sometimes it isn't what we'd rather have, either."

"But you manage to live and grow fat on it just the same," grinned the old servant. "Now your silkworms wouldn't. They'd die, and that would be the end of them. Of course some varieties are more robust than others; but they all have to have the same care."

"I didn't know there was more than one kind of silkworm!" exclaimed Marie in surprise.

"Of course there are," Pierre retorted. "Even I knew that. There are lots of kinds, and some make much better silk than others."

"Some give more silk, too," Josef put in. "Their cocoons are much larger. The big white worm such as we raise here is one of the most profitable. It has four moultings."

"You mean it changes its skin four times?" Marie said.

"Just that. It's a queer life it has, isn't it?" mused the man. "First there is the tiny egg; then comes the caterpillar with all its moultings and its ravenous appetite—then follows the spinning of the cocoons; and the long sleep of the chrysalis, or aurelia, as the slumberer inside the cocoon is sometimes called. And last of all is the moth that comes out of the cocoon—when we will let it—and lays hundreds of eggs for future crops of silkworms. What a short, hard-working life it is!"

"They are funny creatures anyway," observed Pierre thoughtfully. "They don't seem to want to do any of the things other animals do. Silkworms never crawl about as most caterpillars would. Shouldn't you think that after they were hatched they would like to see where they were and would go crawling all round the room?"

"You would think so," replied Josef. "But they don't. They seem to have no wish to move. Perhaps they realize that all their strength must be saved for eating and spinning. Now and then, of course, if they do not find food near at hand when they are first hatched they will bestir themselves until they reach it; they move more at this stage than at any other; and yet they would not move then if they were not hungry. Their chief aim in life seems to be to eat. They are no travelers, that's sure. Even when they emerge from the chrysalis into the moth they use their wings very little, only fluttering a short distance when they are mating."

"But suppose, Josef, that one wants to get them somewhere else and they won't go," speculated Marie.

"Oh, it is easy enough to move them. That can be done any time by means of a good tempting mulberry leaf; they will cling to it tight as a leach and you can cart them round wherever you wish."

"When do you suppose our silkworms will first change their skins, Josef?" asked Pierre.

"Moult?"

"Yes. I forgot the word for it."

"That all depends on the temperature of the room and on how fast they develop. Usually with the degree of heat we keep here the first moulting takes place within eight days. You see your silkworms are only about a quarter of an inch long at first, and as they increase in size to about three inches their skin is not elastic enough to accommodate their rapid growth. It simply won't hold them. Suppose you or Marie grew twelve times your natural size in a few short weeks?"

"I'd pity Mother, letting out our clothes!" chuckled Marie.

"They couldn't be let out; the material wouldn't be there," replied Josef. "And it would be the same way with your skin. It wouldn't stretch. You'd have to have a new one. That's what the silkworm does—only it does it several times over. No skin made can cover an animal that is a quarter of an inch long one week and three-quarters of an inch long the next, and so on growing in leaps and bounds until it gets up to three inches and sometimes more. Think of growing at that rate! And the little gourmands are not eating all the time, either, because after they are hatched it is three days before they eat much. They act stupid, and as if they didn't feel well. But later they make up for their loss of appetite—don't you fret."

Josef smiled grimly.

"By the fourth day they are eating at a furious rate," he went on, "and they keep right on stuffing themselves for five days. When they are about eight days old they have expanded until their skin is so tight that it makes them uncomfortable. It seems to pinch and make them ill. At any rate they act as if they felt pretty poorly and did not want to eat much more. Their next move is to cast their skins. This takes about three or four minutes and is a strenuous business while it lasts; every bit of the old skin goes—even that from the head, jaws, and feet. The ordeal leaves them weak and exhausted, but they soon cheer up, and are eating again furiously as ever. You can't stop them from eating very long."

"How does the new skin look?" inquired Marie. "Just like the other?"

"Why do you ask such foolish questions, Marie?" grumbled Josef. "Haven't you seen your father's silkworms hundreds of times?"

"I'm ashamed to say I never noticed them very much, Josef," returned the girl. "They seemed such horrid little things that I never was interested in them."

"I don't know much about them either," put in Pierre. "I never expected to be raising them myself. If I had I should have examined them more carefully and asked Father lots of questions. It was such a bother always to be gathering mulberry leaves for them that I came to dislike the thought of a silkworm," confessed the boy. "Ever so many times I had to pick leaves when I wanted to go and play. But now, you see, it is different, because they are our own silkworms and of course we want to learn all we can about them. I wish, Josef, you'd please tell us about their new skins."

Josef glanced up good-naturedly.

"If you really want to know of course I'll tell you," he answered. "The new skin looks just about like the old one, except that it is all loose and wrinkled. You know how you look when you are wearing a new suit that your mother has bought for you to grow to, Pierre. Well, that's the way the silkworm's suit looks on him. It is several sizes too big at first. But by the end of five days he has filled it all out until he is as uncomfortable in it as he was in his old one, and is ready for another."

"And he peels this one off just the same way?"

"Just the same—hat, coat, and gloves. This, as I have said, is not at all easy, for you must remember that his skin fits very closely all about his jaws as well as over all his sixteen legs. These are arranged in pairs so when he shifts his skin it is equal to peeling off eight pairs of stockings. How would you like that?"

The boy and girl shook their heads.

"These legs are very nicely planned, too," went on Josef. "There are six in front—three pairs—neatly covered with a thick, shelly coating; these fit under the first three rings of the silkworm's body and can be used as hands when he is spinning. Then come the other ten legs, or holders, which have tiny hooks on them and are the climbing legs."

"But I thought the silkworm scarcely moved," objected Marie.

"Oh, it can move when it wants to. When it gets ready

to spin its cocoon it climbs until it finds a place that suits it. In addition to all these legs it has wonderfully strong jaws. I suppose the good Lord bestowed these upon the silkworm because most of its work in life is done with its jaws—both its eating and spinning. In proportion to its size the silkworm has stronger jaws than any other of the small creatures. Underneath these jaws are two very tiny apertures set close together through which the caterpillar draws and unites into one the two strands of silk. This is sometimes called the spinaret. The silk substance, which is really a yellow gum, passes through the two long glands that run along each side of the silkworm and are fashioned into a single thread in the spinaret."

"And you say the silkworm goes through the process of changing its skin four times, Josef?"

"Yes, four times. You can always tell when it is going to moult, because it raises its head and remains still in that position as if asleep. When it has grown to the full size of its fourth skin it is ready to spin its cocoon. This is all very simple when you understand it; and yet strange and wonderful, too. You'll follow the process more easily when your own silkworms begin to grow and you can watch them go through all these different stages."

"I do hope our silkworms will hatch and develop safely," remarked Pierre anxiously.

"You needn't fear, I guess," was the comforting reply. "I have helped your father hatch out thousands of eggs, and we seldom have had a bit of trouble. I shouldn't worry. By to-morrow or the next day I plan we shall have as fine a crop of silkworms as one could wish to see."

"I hope so—for our sakes and for Father's," said Marie softly.

CHAPTER VI

BUSY DAYS

The Brettons' silkworms hatched as successfully as Josef had foretold they would, and soon Madame Bretton and her boy and girl had all they wished to do. Not that the work was taxing at first. For a while it was a simple matter to gather the fresh young mulberry leaves and keep the juvenile caterpillars amply supplied with food. Even the litter of stems and waste material that had to be cleared away with promptness did not cause much trouble, for most of it fell through the perforations in the tin shelves and could be readily removed. Now and then, of course, some unwary baby silkworm fell through too along with this waste matter and had to be rescued; for the most part, however, the task was simple enough.

"I do not see that it is hard work to raise silkworms," announced Pierre at the end of the first few days. "Why, a six-year-old child could feed them! It is the easiest thing imaginable."

Josef laughed.

"Just you wait, Pierre Bretton!" was his retort. "Some day in the near future I'll remind you of those words. The first three weeks are not arduous, I'll agree. The next twelve or fourteen days are harder, though; there are more things to think of and more food to gather. And as for the last part of the time—it demands all the care and labor that you will wish to expend."

But Pierre only shrugged his shoulders sceptically.

In the meantime the silkworms continued to thrive. The weather was warm and sunny and no irregular conditions broke in upon the work until one afternoon Josef announced in a warning tone:

"There'll be rain to-morrow. You better gather double your supply of mulberry leaves; for if you wait until morning the trees will be dripping wet, so we cannot find food for our caterpillars."

It was a timely forecast, for the old servant's prediction proved a true one, and thanks to his thoughtfulness, the crop of the youthful sericulturists escaped famine. After that the silk-raisers kept their eyes out for the possibility of showers or stormy weather. Never for an hour did they run out of food to supply the busy little creatures that were to earn for the Bretton family a livelihood. Tirelessly they fed the caterpillars; tirelessly cleared away the litter that it might not ferment and cause malady, or bury the worms beneath its weight and render them hot and torpid. For it was by keeping them vigorous and alert, with plenty of fresh food and fresh air that they would develop the heartiest appetite, grow the fastest, and spin the largest cocoons. All these points were too important to be overlooked. Whenever the litter accumulated too fast or failed to drop through the grating of the shelves the caterpillars were gently removed on a cluster of fresh mulberry leaves to another spot, and the place made clean and tidy.

Then came a day when the silkworms began to cease eating and instead paused idly, with heads upraised.

"They are ready for their first moulting!" exclaimed Josef. "They want to peel off their tight clothing. Watch and see if I am not right."

And sure enough! The great transformation took place even as the old servant had said it would. Off came the skins—cap, shoes, and all!

The boy and girl were delighted.

After the poor, fatigued, wrinkled caterpillars had wriggled themselves free from their hampering garments they were sorry looking creatures indeed! But with a little rest they roused themselves and were soon eating voraciously, just as if nothing had happened. Day by day their appetites increased, and to keep pace with them they grew longer and plumper.

Again they shed their skins, and again were back eating as ravenously as before.

"The wrinkles surely do not have a chance to stay long in their coats," remarked Pierre. "Pretty soon they will want still other larger coats, too."

Full-sized leaves with a more solid fibre were now demanded by the maturing silkworms; but Josef cautioned the silk-raisers not to give their little charges old or tough leaves.

"There is a big difference between full grown vegetation,

and old passé stuff," he explained. "You know how tired your jaws get chewing tough food. Well, theirs do, too. Remember they chew day in and day out—nights as well as other times. You've got to conserve their strength, for they will need every bit of it before they finish their work. I knew of some silkworms once that died from sheer exhaustion because they were given food that was too tough for them to masticate. It is not an uncommon happening."

As the caterpillars continued to eat without cessation the odd little sound of the cutting of crisp leaves pervaded the silk-house. It was no such easy task to keep them supplied with food now! Day after day it was a race to pick the necessary quantity of leaves and remove the accumulating litter. Every one in the house worked, and even a boy or two was hired to help in the gathering.

"It is not so easy now, eh?" suggested Josef to Pierre. "Getting tired?"

"A little," admitted the boy. "It keeps one so on the everlasting jump. Taking away the litter is stupid, tedious work; and then there is the double supply of leaves to last through the night!"

He sighed.

"You're right. It is a hard job," the old servant agreed kindly. "But have courage. When you get your first crop of fine cocoons you will say it was worth it all, and you will forget that you ever were tired."

"I hope so," murmured Pierre wearily. "I get discouraged standing and hearing them gnaw those leaves. I know they are just making more work for us."

"You'd have far more cause to be disheartened if you didn't

hear them," chuckled Josef. "That would be something to mourn over. But you shouldn't complain at their good healthy appetites."

Cheered by Josef's jests the work went on.

The endless monotony of feeding and clearing up, feeding and clearing up continued. Sometimes it seemed as if nothing was being accomplished. And yet when the young silk-growers compared the present size of their silkworms with that of the early hatched caterpillars the transformation seemed nothing short of a miracle.

Then came a day when Pierre detected a change in the aspect of his crop. Gradually the worms had turned to a transparent green color and ceasing to eat were moving uneasily about. They seemed also to have shrunk to a smaller size.

In consternation the lad fled to Josef.

"Whatever is the matter with them?" he cried. "Are they ill? Has some epidemic come at this late day to sweep away all that we have done?"

The boy's face was pale with distress.

"They're all right," answered Josef reassuringly. "They are just ready to spin, that's all. I did not expect it quite so soon. We must get the arches up without delay."

Both Pierre and Marie clapped their hands. They knew well what was to happen next for they had often seen their father arrange the little arches of brush on which the silkworms were to climb and spin their cocoons. The placing of these rustic half-hoops was a delicate matter, since it was necessary to arrange them so that plenty of air might circulate through the space they enclosed; otherwise the worms would refuse to spin. Twigs or slender pieces of brush were set along the shelves in such a way that when bent the shelf above held them in place and made of them a series of miniature bridges, or arches. For certain varieties of caterpillars Pierre gathered branches of oak shoots with dried leaves clinging to them because Josef explained that this type of silkworm preferred that sort of twig on which to fashion its cocoon; other brush was stripped of leaves. And throughout the following days the greatest care had to be taken that nothing should interrupt the spinning.

The things most to be dreaded were sudden noises; thunder-storms; and above all a drop in temperature, since chilly surroundings congealed the fluid silk in the ducts at each side of the silkworm, rendering it too thick for the creature to spin into fibre.

The noise and the temperature could to an extent be controlled. But the thunder-storms! Those were another matter.

Anxiously the Bretton family studied every passing cloud.

"If a severe storm should wreck our crop now—at the very end—it would be cruel!" declared Pierre. "No matter how careful we are we cannot prevent some great black thunder-head from rolling over the mountains and down through the valley."

"It is useless to worry, dear," answered his mother. "If such a storm comes it will be through no fault of ours."

"It would raise havoc in our harvest just the same," cut in Josef. "The vibrations of thunder sound worse among the metal shelves. They catch the jar, and seem to hold and echo it. Your father told me about a man near Tours who had lightning wires along his shelves to protect his silkworms from electric currents. The wires carried off the worst of the vibration."

"I wish we could afford to equip our silk-house that way," said Marie.

"Just wait until we get rich. Maybe some day we can," answered Pierre gaily.

Fortunately for the Brettons' silkworms, however, no electrical storm came.

The caterpillars climbed serenely into the brush arches above their heads, selected spots that pleased their fancy, and began constructing their cocoons. First came the loose, web-like oval within which the cocoon itself was to be made. This was the work of the first day and its construction was of what is known as floss. Then followed the yellow, compact cocoon requiring three or four days for its spinning. Occasionally two worms would insist upon spinning together, crossing and recrossing their threads; these double cocoons always had to be sorted out from the others, however, as the silk could not be wound off them easily.

The spinning was an interesting sight.

The silkworms poised themselves on the lower extremity of their bodies and using their front legs to guide the thread, sent it hither and thither from their mouths in wavy, irregular motion until the little egg-shaped ball was finished. The two fibres from the right and left side of the worm were so perfectly united in the spinaret that it was impossible to detect more than one thread. Patiently the tiny spinners toiled, and those worms that failed to spin were put into a room by themselves where the temperature was graded to a higher degree of heat that the warmer atmosphere might stimulate them to work.

When at last the cocoons were done the Brettons surveyed them with satisfaction.

The weeks had been busy, fatiguing ones with hastily snatched meals, and interrupted slumbers.

"One could not keep on like this for a long stretch without more help," declared Madame Bretton. "I am glad the caterpillars have their houses made!"

"They are better houses than you think, too," added Josef. "For each silkworm has coated the inside of his little home with a gum-like substance that makes it waterproof. He has no intention of lying down to sleep in a leaky cottage where the rain may drip through."

"But there is no rain in here," objected Marie.

"Of course not. But the silkworm does not know that. He builds his house just as he would if it was out-of-doors where the good Lord intended it should be. Your caterpillar hasn't the wit to realize that conditions have changed with the years, and that he now lives out his days beneath a roof that does away with the need of water-proofing. It is because the cocoons are thus sealed on the inside that the water does not penetrate them when they are floated. You'll notice that if you ever have a chance to see the silk reeled off. It protects the chrysalis until it pierces its way through its silken house and comes out a moth. But of course we shall not let ours do that."

"Why not?" inquired Marie.

"Why not? Because after you have worked so hard to get your silk you do not want it broken into short bits and spoiled, do you? If we were to let the moths mature and make holes in the cocoons it would ruin all our silk. No. We must let only a few moths come out and lay their eggs that we may have them to hatch for our next crop of silkworms. We'll select some of the finest cocoons for the purpose—those that are largest and most perfect. Some must be male and some must be female moths."

"But how can we tell? Aren't they all shut up inside the cocoons?" gasped Pierre.

"Oh, it is quite easy," answered Josef. "The female silkworm spins a house which, like an egg, is a little sharper at one end than at the other. We'll choose about the same number of each gender. There is a knack in selecting good cocoons for breeding, and you've got to know lots of things about them. And after we have chosen them there will be the rest of the cocoons to sort. That will require care, too. We cannot do it as experts do, but still we can group them roughly into lots of various kinds. We can get at it to-morrow. I will give you your first lesson. I fancy your mother knows more about it than the rest of us for she has always helped your father do this part of the work."

"It will be fun to learn!" cried Marie. "Won't it, Pierre?"

"I don't believe it will be very hard," sniffed Pierre. "There can't be much choice in cocoons. Most of them look alike, except that some are bigger than others."

Josef regarded the boy a moment and then laughed.

"Don't be too cock-sure of that!" he retorted ironically.

CHAPTER VII

THE SILK HARVEST

he Bretton family spent the next week collecting and sorting their cocoons into baskets, grouping together as well as they were able those that were to be kept for breeding; those that were soiled or imperfect; and those that were double. They also separated the cocoons that were of different colors, for among the lot were not only white ones but many that were yellow, and even some of a greenish tint. This varied, Josef explained, with the different species of silkworms. Before the silk was reeled off the cocoons would, of course, go through another and more thorough classification under the hands of the experts at the filature, as the reeling factory was called. But even this first rough grouping was a help to the buyers.

In the meantime some of the caterpillars that worked more slowly were still busy with their spinning, and could not be disturbed. Accordingly much care had to be taken in removing the cocoons that were finished. Those in the lower tiers of arches were first taken out, and afterward the ones higher up on the shelves. The sooner the cocoons could be collected, after their completion, Josef said, the better, for within ten days they depreciated from seven to eight percent, and if sold in bulk, brought a lower price. In consequence the Brettons, who were to sell their crop to a silk merchant who visited the town each year, promptly set about gathering their harvest as soon as possible.

Many of the cocoons were really beautiful, being of a perfect oval outline and of pale golden color.

Marie and Pierre were delighted.

"It is worth all the endless trays of mulberry leaves, isn't it, Mother?" exclaimed Marie. "Why, even Father could raise no finer or larger cocoons, I am sure."

"We have done well," her mother agreed. "But remember, we have had great good luck. No epidemic or disease came to blight the lives of our caterpillars; nor did annoyances of any sort interrupt their spinning. We did our part, certainly; but favorable conditions had much to do with our success."

"I only hope we have kept the right sort of cocoons for breeding," said Josef. "That is all that is troubling me now. Upon our selection will depend the quality of our next season's crop. There are so many things to think of in choosing cocoons for hatching. Not only must they be as perfect as we can get them, but they must have nicely rounded ends and a fine, strong thread. I tried to search out those with the ring-like band round the centre, for I have heard your father say that if we could get those we would be sure of having vigorous silkworms, since only caterpillars of the most powerful constitution make their houses in that way."

"It seems to me we kept out a lot more than we shall need for breeding, Josef," complained Marie.

"We always have to put aside more than we actually require, Marie, because many will fail to hatch successfully and will be a loss," explained Josef. "Usually growers plan to devote about a sixth of their crop to this purpose."

"A sixth! Why, that would cut down our sales dreadfully!" ejaculated the girl.

"Better sell less now and be assured of a plentiful supply of eggs next year," was the dry answer. "Don't you think so?"

Therefore the cocoons for hatching were gathered into one place and after the floss that clung to the outside of them had been removed so that it should not entangle the moth when it came forth from its house, Madame Bretton took a needle and being extremely careful not to pierce the chrysalis inside by putting it through the centre of the cocoons she strung them on strings from three to four feet long and hung them over some wires stretched across the top of the room.

"There!" she said. "Nothing can reach them now. They will be well up out of the way of both mice and chickens, and in a month or two should hatch out all right."

The weather in the meantime had become very hot. The southern sun beat down on Bellerivre, parching its hillsides, and tanning its people to a dusky brown. But the peasants complained not of the high temperature, for was not this torrid sun that burned so fiercely the very factor they were calculating upon to complete for them the final preparation of their cocoons for the market? This consisted in killing the chrysalis, or sleeping worm inside the cocoon, lest it come out and snap the delicate threads that it had spun. In cooler countries the process was accomplished by putting baskets of cocoons covered with paper and wrapped in cloth into ovens about hot enough for the baking of bread. Here they were left an hour or so until all moisture had exuded from them, proving that the worm had been dried up. Sometimes a blast of steam-heat was the method used for the destruction of the chrysalis. Such methods required greatest care, however, lest in employing a degree of heat sufficient to exterminate the worm the silk also be damaged. But in Bellerivre no such artificial means had to be resorted to. Instead the cocoons were spread out beneath the burning rays of the sun and left to bake, being wrapped each night in heavy black cloth that had also absorbed the heat and would retain during the night the high temperature acquired through the day. For three days this process was continued, the cocoons being spread in the sun from dawn until dusk, and then bundled up inside the hot cloth throughout the night.

On the fourth day Josef said:

"Now it is time that we investigated and found out whether the worms are really dead."

He thereupon took a few cocoons and cutting them open proceeded to examine the chrysalis inside. It was motionless and dry. Again he looked at it, this time touching it with the point of a needle. Still it did not move.

"It is quite dead," he remarked. "And the others must be so too. What wonder, when they have been so steadily exposed to this broiling sun? I should be dead if I were to lie in it day after day without protection, and so would you. We can now safely gather the lot into baskets and put them away until Monsieur Leclerq, the buyer, comes for them at the end of the week."

So once again the cocoons were collected to await their purchaser, and the silk-raisers sat down with sighs of content to anticipate the payment of the money they had so faithfully earned, and speculate as to what they should do with it.

"I don't believe you are any more glad to rest than your silkworms are!" reflected Josef. "When you consider that each one of them spins between three and four hundred yards of thread you can't blame it for wanting to sleep when its work is done."

"Do they spin as much as that?" gasped Marie.

"Indeed they do—some of them more. Certain of the finest varieties will even turn out as many as six hundred and twenty-five yards. But that is a high figure. They usually average less."

"It is all wonderful, isn't it?" replied Madame Bretton. "And to think these tiny creatures are responsible for the silk the whole world uses!"

"I know it," agreed Josef. "Of course there are other spinners in the universe, however. The spider, for example, is a most industrious spinner, and I have read that in the past scientists tried to see if some of the larger spiders could not be utilized for silk-making. The velvety pouch, or bag, was removed and by some skilful process the greyish thread inside it was carded off. But the experiment was unsuccessful, for the silk thus made was far less firm and strong than that which came from the silkworm. After this failure another set of men tried to make silk by using the filament of the pinna."

"What is a pinna, Josef?" questioned Marie.

"The pinna is a variety of shell-fish not unlike the mussel; it fastens itself to the rocks and from between its shells gives out threads something like those of the spider or silkworm. By means of them it spins a tough fibre by which it joins itself to any object to which it wishes to cling."

"And did they succeed in making pinna silk, Josef?" demanded Marie eagerly.

"They certainly did!" nodded Josef. "Along the Mediterranean were several places where they manufactured pinna thread. They even spun some fine, silky fabrics from it. But they never could get enough of the filament to make the industry practical, although in 1754 they did send to Pope Benedict XIV some stockings made from pinna silk. They were spun from very fine thread, and were so closely woven and so hot that I doubt if he cared to wear them unless in cool weather. Since then the weaving of pinna silk has been abandoned, although now and then one sees bits of it in some old fabric, or on exhibition somewhere. It is chiefly regarded as a curiosity."

"What a lot you know, Josef!" murmured Marie, astonished.

Josef laughed.

"I just happened to see that in a book your father gave me," he said. "It interested me because it told of something I wanted to learn about. I don't care for reading as a rule. Most books are about things I never heard of and are no use to me."

"But don't you like to learn about new things?" inquired Marie.

"Why, no, I don't think I do. What good is it?" interrogated the old servant. "I'm not ever going out of this valley. Why, I'm 'most seventy years old already! It is well enough for you to learn things—you're young. As for me, the learning I have has stood by me up to now, and I guess it will do me the rest of my days."

With a smile on his simple face the venerable man turned away.

CHAPTER VIII

PIERRE MAKES A FRIEND

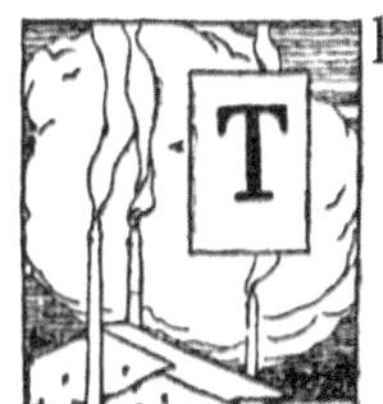

The buyer who came to Bellerivre from the Gaspard silk mills was a lively little Frenchman whom Pierre had often seen before.

"So it is you, my young friend, who this year raises the cocoons!" cried the merchant cordially. "Who would have thought it possible? But yesterday you were a baby in your father's arms. And now——" the little man shrugged his shoulders. "Eh bien, le bon chien chasse de race! N'est pas, Madame?"

Madame Bretton smiled.

"The lad is but doing his best to fill his father's place," she answered quietly.

"That is as it should be with all good French boys, too," the merchant assented. "And have you ever visited our silk mills at Pont-de-Saint-Michel? No? Ah, but you should do so. It is only an hour's journey, and if you are to raise silk you must learn all you can about it. If I should give you a letter to our foreman would not Madame, your mother, be willing you should go?"

Pierre glanced up eagerly.

His eyes sparkled.

"Would you, Mother? It would not cost very much, would it?" He turned apologetically to the silk buyer. "You see," he explained, "in these war days we must be very saving, for every franc that we can spare goes to my father and my uncle, who are in the army."

"I know," sighed the agent. "Wherever I go it is the same. All the men are at the front. But the cost of the trip I suggested is very little, and I myself should be glad to——"

"No, Monsieur Leclerq," interrupted Madame Bretton. "I know what you would say, and I thank you; but we are well able to pay Pierre's expenses to Saint Michel, since you are so kind as to invite him. I am sure the excursion would more than repay us. It would not be like taking the money for a mere pleasure tour. Pierre shall go. It will be another step toward making a silk merchant of him."

"I wish I could go, too," whispered Marie.

"You are not to be a silk merchant, chérie," answered her mother gently. "We women are the stay-at-homes, who do all we can to help our men forward in their careers; that is our work."

And so the next day Pierre, very happy and important, and with a large box of luncheon under his arm, set out upon the train for the Pont-de-Saint-Michel silk mills. To be going on such a long journey all alone was a novel undertaking for the lad, who seldom left his own green valley. It was almost as wonderful as if he were starting for Marseilles, or indeed Paris itself. The place where he was going did not, however, possess the glamour of either of these great cities. On the contrary it was merely a sort of depot or centre to which all the cocoons bought up in the vicinity were sent to have the silk reeled from them; there were also at this plant some extensive throwing mills, but no weaving was done there. Instead the thrown silk was sold to the great weaving factories at Lyons, Tours, or other silk-making cities of France; and the raw product was sent to Marseilles, from which market it was either distributed to French mills or shipped to England or the United States for manufacture.

The day was a beautiful one. Massive white clouds hung low over the distant mountains; but the valley was flooded with golden sunshine that illumined it like some vast search-light. The vineyards never looked greener, the hillsides more velvety and cool, or the river more sparkling. Now the train skirted the banks of the stream, now shot past meadows of fertile farming land; or of a sudden it crossed a noisy mountain torrent and crept up the hillside until the vegetation became low and stunted, and the rocky peaks of the Pyrenees seemed but an arm's length away. Then slowly down over a trestle of airily poised bridge-work it descended to the valley again. Was ever a journey such a marvel? To the French boy who had seen little of the outside world it was an Arabian Night's dream.

All too soon Saint Michel was reached, and Pierre set out for the silk mills, where he presented the card that Monsieur Leclerq had given him. Then for a few minutes he waited in a small office where the jar of machinery and the whirr of wheels caused a monotonous and unceasing vibration.

Presently a giant foreman with sleeves rolled to the elbow came hurrying out.

He regarded Pierre with surprise.

"They told me that one of our silk-growers wanted to see me," faltered he uncertainly. "There has doubtless been some mistake. You are but a boy."

"I am nevertheless a silk-grower," smiled Pierre modestly. "It is because the men of our household are in the trenches that I——"

Impulsively the foreman thrust out his hand.

"I too have relatives in the battle line," he said. "My brother and cousins are there, and I should be with them now were it not for an ugly wound I got at the Marne. They will not take me back to fight, even though I have begged to go. And so here I am—restless and half angry that I must remain boxed up at Saint Michel and make silk instead of being where the firing is going on. Yet some must stay behind and carry on the country's industries. Perhaps I can still do my bit here. I have tried to be philosophical about it and work as hard as I can, for I feel that those who cannot help in one way can, maybe, help in another."

He glanced at the card Pierre had brought.

"Bretton is your name?"

"Pierre Bretton."

"Monsieur Leclerq says your shipment of cocoons was a good contribution to the prosperity of France."

Pierre flushed.

"I am glad if it seemed so. We must support ourselves—my mother, sister, and I—and not be a burden to the country while my father is away."

"That's the right spirit," answered the foreman heartily. "And so you want to see your silk reeled off—yours, or somebody's else? Well, you shall. I am busy myself and so cannot go with you; but Henri, one of our boys, shall take you with him and tell you all you wish to know. Do not fear to ask questions if you do not understand, for Henri is well able to answer them. He knows everything that anybody can about silk reeling."

As he beckoned to a tall, slender boy who sat at a desk opposite, the foreman smiled kindly down at Pierre.

"Henri," he continued when the employee approached, "I want you to show this young silk-raising friend of ours, Monsieur Bretton, how we sort cocoons and reel them off. Tell him everything you can, for he is a grower and has the right to know."

"Mais, oui, avec beaucoup de plaisir," answered the boy. "I will do my best." He bowed to the foreman, who, after shaking Pierre by the hand, turned away. "Now Monsieur Bretton——"

"My name is Pierre. No one ever called me Monsieur Bretton before, and I do not like it," protested Pierre smiling. "I am but a boy like yourself. Please call me by my first name—if you do not mind."

Henri beamed on him.

"I should like it much better," he replied cordially. "And I am Henri St. Amant. Now it is all understood, is it not? Shall we begin then our journey through the filature? We will go into the sorting rooms first, where the cocoons that are sent to us are classified. Most of them have already been cured, or baked, for the majority of our customers do that for us. When they do not we have to expose the cocoons in our own ovens."

HE LED THE WAY INTO A LONG ROOM

"Don't most of your cocoons come to you sorted?" questioned Pierre.

"Most of them are roughly classified," nodded Henri. "But the grading must be much more finely done. Only experts can sort cocoons thoroughly."

As he spoke he led the way into a long room, where on every hand girls were moving in and out among heaps of cocoons that were either piled high on tables or massed upon squares of canvas on the floor. The room and everything in it was spotless.

"We try to keep the cocoons from getting soiled, you see," explained Henri.

"Is the sorting done by girls?" questioned Pierre, astonished.

"Since the war, yes. We have had to train them to take the places of those who have gone to be soldiers. It is not, of course, heavy work, but it requires skill and judgment since the many varieties of cocoons need different treatment. Here, for example, are dupions, or double cocoons, which as you doubtless already know have more floss on the outside than do others, and must be well cleaned before any attempt at reeling can be made. Often they cannot be run off at all because the two caterpillars that worked together to make the single cocoon have intertwined the threads until they break all to bits when we try to separate them. Here is another species of cocoon." Henri pointed to a pile on the next table. "These are of beautiful texture, smooth and satiny. But they must be treated with tepid, not hot, water, as are a good proportion of the others, and the accumulation of gum mixed with the filament must be soaked out with soap-suds. This will give you an idea how many things there are to think of in reeling.

Some cocoons give off their silk too easily, and unless put into cool water will snarl; others fail to give off the thread at all and instead must be treated with hot water, which aids in loosening it. Another difficulty we sometimes encounter is that the reelers cannot catch the end of the thread to begin their work; this usually indicates that the water into which the cocoons have been put is too cool. On the other hand if the silk ruffs up and comes off in snarls upon the brush, the matted masses indicate that the water is too hot. All this the reelers must learn by experience, and they must learn it, too, without wasting our silk. Two general laws underlie this feature of silk-reeling: hot water makes the silk run faster, and cold water retards its progress. Your problem is to see which treatment your cocoons require."

"Of course those who sort the cocoons can tell nothing of that," ventured Pierre.

"Oh, no. The sorters simply put into one place those cocoons that are of the same kind. The way the cocoons behave in the water is the business of the reeler. We have tanks or basins of a graduated temperature, and the operators soon learn into which one to put a cocoon of a certain type."

"I did not dream one had to know so much just to reel off the silk," murmured Pierre. "I had always supposed it would be an easy matter; but now I see it isn't."

Henri laughed.

"But I have not told you half our troubles yet," he answered mischievously. "Thus far I have spoken only of the cocoons. In addition there is the water to consider. That must be the right sort, too. It must be as pure as we can get it, both chemically and in color. And even then the high temperature necessary to bring the silk off the cocoons will cause any sandy sediment there may be in it to rise to the surface and cut the filament as we reel it off. We have to be prepared for that emergency as well as the others. And now to return to the sorting of the cocoons. Do you see that pile over there? Those are what we call perfect ones. The thread from them will go into the finest quality silks and satins, as the filament has neither spots nor flaws."

"But those cocoons are very small," objected Pierre.

"Yes. The best cocoons are not always the largest, by any means. It is quality, not size, that counts." Henri passed on. "Here now," he continued as he paused before another lot, "are some more pointed at one end than at the other. We know from bitter experience that they will reel badly, because the silk which runs smoothly at the beginning will prove to be weak in some places and break. We toss them aside and reel them separately. These *cocalons*, as we call this other kind, are also thrown out because they are hard to wind."

"They are much larger," observed Pierre.

"You are right. Nevertheless they have no more silk on them. The reason they look bigger is because the worm spun them less compactly; unless they are put into cold water they will tangle and mat when reeled."

"And that next lot?"

"*Soufflons?* They are the most imperfect cocoon made. The silk is so loosely spun that it cannot be wound at all, and is good only for floss."

Pierre shook his head despairingly.

"I thought I knew quite a lot about cocoons," he said. "But by the time I go home I shall feel I don't know anything. Why,

I never could learn to sort all those kinds if I kept trying for years."

"Only those who have handled thousands of cocoons can," returned his guide consolingly. "I couldn't begin to do it. Here is a pile now! They have a hole in the end and cannot be reeled because every time the thread comes to the perforation it is broken. Probably the moth was allowed to escape and injured the filament. They must be used for floss, too, for they are good for nothing else."

The boys wandered on down the room.

"In this pile you will see what we call *good choquettes*," resumed Henri. "I must tell you about them, for the species is peculiar. The worm inside them died before finishing its work and stuck onto the inside of the cocoon." He took one from the heap and shook it. "It does not rattle, you see. Nevertheless the filament on it is of excellent quality—not very strong, perhaps, but of fine texture. In contrast to these good choquettes is this tableful of *bad choquettes*. Like the others the silkworm died during his spinning, but this time he rotted away inside, leaving the cocoon black and mottled."

"Healthy worms make the best cocoons, of course," Pierre rejoined.

"Not at all," contradicted Henri. "Here is what is known as a calcined cocoon made by a worm which had a peculiar disease that turned it to powder. You would not think that such a creature could spin the best quality of silk there is, would you? Yet it is so. Listen to the queer rattle the cocoon has."

Holding it to Pierre's ear he shook it gently.

"These cocoons not only have excellent silk on them, but they have more of it than if they had been spun by a healthy worm. As a result they command the highest price and buyers are eager to find them."

"I guess I don't know anything about silkworms or cocoons either," announced Pierre in dismay.

Both boys laughed.

"It is amazing how much there is to know about almost anything when you once start to learn about it from top to bottom," declared Henri. "I came into this filature when quite young, and it has taken me years to find out even the little I know now."

"I think you know a lot," Pierre returned admiringly. "I'd be happy if I knew even half as much."

"Oh, no you wouldn't," was the prompt retort. "You'd want to know a great deal more, just as I do—that is, if you were any good. There are a thousand things I want to find out. The silk business, you see, is to be my trade. I have an uncle in the weaving mills at Lyons, and some day when I know more he is to find a place for me there. So I am learning all I can about the classifying and reeling of cocoons; and I have also raised a few silkworms so as to be familiar with the very beginnings of the industry. Soon I am to go into the filature to help with the reeling; and after that they have promised to send me on into the throwing mills, where the filament is twisted into thread preparatory to weaving. Then I shall be ready to go to Lyons and see how silks, satins, and velvets are made. Lyons, you know, is a famous silk-making city. It was there that Philippe de la Salle, the great silk designer, lived. Because he did such beautiful work he was decorated by Louis XVI with the Order of Saint Michel and was given a pension of six mille livres. Think of that! Alas, such things do not happen now. That was long ago—between 1723 and 1803. His good fortune did not, however, last long, for the Revolution came, and the court which gave him his money went out of power. Still the people of Lyons were proud of him and despite the fact that he had been a court favorite they provided for him lodgings in the Palais Saint Pierre, where he lived for the rest of his life."

"I am afraid I do not know much about what he did," said Pierre with engaging frankness.

"Why, it was Philippe de la Salle who designed the silk hangings for the chamber of Marie Antoinette, and who originated the Empire motif of the wreath of laurel; he also designed silks gorgeous with garlands intertwined with ribbon; or decorated with baskets of fruit and flowers; and sometimes he made use of great birds. He has done some of the finest silk designs ever woven. My uncle told me, however, that years and years before that wonderful silks were made; and that fragments showing beautiful designs are in the museums of Berlin and Nuremberg, as well as in our own Cluny Museum, and the great museums of London. He said there were also marvelous church vestments of even earlier date and also some very ancient Byzantine silks splendid with griffins, eagles, and lions. Some day, perhaps, I shall go to see them, and maybe I myself may learn to weave such fabrics. Who knows? And what are you going to do, Pierre?"

"I suppose I shall just go on raising silkworms," was the quiet reply. "It is hard work, but I see nothing else ahead for me. However, when my father and uncle return from the war there will be time enough for me to think what I will do."

"Ah, but you have a plan already; I can see that!" Henri cried.

Pierre nodded gravely.

"Yes, I have a plan—or perhaps I better call it a dream. I should like to go to America. One can earn more money there. My mother's brother is at Paterson, New Jersey, which is in America, and I have some young cousins there also."

"Yes, yes, I know," exclaimed Henri eagerly. "There are great silk mills at Paterson where they make fine silks and ribbons—some of them as beautiful as any we make in France. Maybe some day you will go there."

"I'm afraid not," returned Pierre. "Even should the war end and my father and uncle come home again I have no money to go to America."

"Don't give up so easily," Henri said, placing a hand on the younger boy's shoulder. "We never can tell what will happen. My mother says that if we do the best we can every day sometimes the thing we wish most will come to us; if not, Le Bon Dieu will send something else which may be even better."

"I am trying to do my best," Pierre answered bravely. "And anyway so long as my father and uncle are safe nothing else really matters."

The boys exchanged a smile and passed on into the filature, as the factory where the reeling was done was called.

CHAPTER IX

HENRI MAKES A SUGGESTION

It is now dry weather, and as this is the best time to reel silk we are working very hard," explained Henri as they went along. "Every machine we have is running overtime. But before we inspect the reels themselves suppose we see how the cocoons are soaked and made ready. The important thing is to get the gum which the silkworm has blended with the silk out of it, and for this purpose we use soft water, having found that it loosens the filament better than anything else. That is what they are doing here. They begin by raising the water to the boiling point, and afterward reduce its temperature by means of cold water if they find it necessary. Care must be taken to submerge each cocoon evenly so that its entire surface will be covered; otherwise one end will be softened and the other end remain hard, in which case it cannot be reeled off."

"But why do the girls stir the cocoons with those whisks of peeled birch?" inquired Pierre curiously. "What are they trying to do?"

"The stirring frees the ends of the filaments, and the brush of twigs serves to collect them," answered Henri. "When the ends have been caught in this way they are passed on to the reeler; but if after trying this method the girls find the ends do not free themselves they put such cocoons into a different temperature of water, or else toss them out entirely and leave them to the employees who handle the lots that require special treatment. They cannot stop here to fuss with cocoons that fail to wind off readily; not only would such troublesome ones retard the work, but they would be likely to snarl the others. Frequently we find cocoons with uneven places in the thread, spots where the silkworm has been interrupted in its spinning and stopped, afterward going on with its work and making a lump or knob where the filament has been joined. Such cocoons wind badly, as you can well imagine, and they, too, cannot be reeled with the general lot."

"I notice those boys are taking the empty cocoons out of the tanks after the silk has been reeled from them. Is it necessary?"

"Yes. We never allow the discarded cocoons, or shells as we call them, to stand in the water with those that are soaking, because they not only spoil the sheen of the silk on the unreeled cocoons but discolor it," Henri replied. "Now let us watch the reeling. Shall we?"

The boys turned toward the whirling machinery.

"I had no idea they reeled so fast," declared Pierre, speaking loudly so his companion could hear.

Fascinated he stood watching the flying threads pass over the glass rods.

"The speed of the reels can be regulated, of course," answered Henri. "It is not often, though, that the filament snaps because the reel is moving too fast. When the thread does break it is more frequently because the regular motion of the machinery wears it until it parts. This cannot always be avoided. All filatures count on some loss by winding. But the percentage in a modernly equipped filature is very small. We use the glass rods to prevent the thread from being caught or roughened. The process of winding cocoons has been so carefully studied that now our French reelers can turn off silk of fifteen or twenty fibres and lose only one or two percent of it by waste. In Turkey the loss runs as high as six or eight percent; in Syria it is fifteen or twenty percent; and in other countries where the people have less mechanical skill the rate of loss is much higher. Successful silk reeling is a matter of good machinery, practice, and deftness. An experienced reeler knows his business too well to waste material."

"All this is amazing to me," said Pierre. "I thought the men just took the end of the thread and wound it off without any trouble."

Henri shook his head.

"No, indeed. I wish it were as easy as that. A reeler needs judgment, judgment, judgment at every turn. Not only must the floss be removed from the outside of the cocoon before it is reeled, but also the first part of the filament, which usually is weak and too fine for use, must be wound off until the firm, strong thread is reached. You see, the caterpillar has to work a little while before it gets under way and does its best spinning. All that poor filament on which it experiments or gets started must be broken off and saved for embroidery floss, since it is fit neither to be woven into broad goods or twisted into sewing silk. The reeler begins to wind where the end of the filament becomes strong. He then must combine enough fibres of the same size and strength to make a thread uniform in size. And this is not so easy as it sounds, since there is great diversity in the coarseness and fineness of the filament on the cocoons. He cannot always put the same number of filaments together. In addition to this fact he is often required to reel silk of various sizes. The coarseness or fineness demanded all depends on the purpose for which the silk is to be used. But always each kind must be of uniform size throughout."

"And how does he join the fresh cocoons to the others? By tying?"

"No. He runs them in so skilfully that the joining cannot be detected. Every moment he must be on the watch to add new filaments when he sees any of his cocoons giving out. As one cocoon takes the place of another its filament blends unnoticed in the thread. You can see that it would never do to join a lot of new ones all in the same spot."

"I suppose the cocoons run in uneven lengths, anyway, don't they?" ventured Pierre. "Scarcely any of them would contain the same number of yards of filament even were they all to be started together."

"Precisely. So the reeler keeps adding fresh fibres, being careful always that his thread is running uniform all the time. If he uses fibres of fine quality there must be more of them; if coarser fibres not so many. He can't turn out thread that is thick in one place and thin in another."

"That is what you or I would do," laughed Pierre. "Or at least I should. I never could reel so fast, either."

"It winds better fast," replied Henri. "It has not so much time to loosen or get caught. It just has to keep moving right along. If we can get cocoons soon enough so they can be wound off before the moth has time to come out, instead of having them cured first, they reel far more easily. The curing affects the silk. Of course in most cases it is unavoidable, for it would require very quick work for our agents to buy up the products of outlying silk-raisers and get them to us before the chrysalis matured. We should be taking a big chance of having our silk ruined, since one never can predict exactly how long it will be before the moth will come out. Varying conditions bring different results. It is a pity, however, that they have to be cured. Still, the curing has one advantage—it decreases the weight of the cocoons about twenty-five percent."

"I didn't realize that curing caused shrinkage."

"Oh my, yes. And perhaps you did not know what a difference there is in the weight of individual cocoons. This depends not alone on the species of silkworm raised, but also on the care that has been given it. A carefully fed caterpillar will grow larger and make a bigger cocoon. The same law holds with well cultivated flowers or with well tended live stock. Even persons show the results of proper nourishment. It is just so with silkworms. Cultivation tells. And not only does good care result in larger caterpillars and finer cocoons, but also in more silk. So the number of cocoons necessary to total a pound of raw silk vary. We cannot compute that, except roughly. But we do estimate that broadly speaking it takes about an acre of full grown mulberry trees to produce forty pounds of raw silk."

"How interesting!" exclaimed Pierre. "I never thought of measuring silk in mulberry trees."

"Not precisely in trees, but in their leaves," corrected Henri. "If you were a scientific sericulturist, as many men are, you would know just how many pounds of leaves you used each day; and you would work to economize them so as to get the largest possible yield of silk from the smallest possible outlay of leaves. All the big silk-growers manage their business that way."

Pierre sighed.

"My mother said that too," he returned. "But you see, we do not know enough to plan things so closely. However, it does not make much difference, for we have plenty of mulberry trees. With the number of silkworms we raise we never could use them all up. Years ago my father set out our grove, and each season he has added new trees to it until now it stretches from behind our house far down to the river."

"It would bring you in a lot of money if you ever wanted to sell it."

"Sell it!"

"Yes."

"But we'd never sell it!" retorted Pierre. "Pray, how should we live if we gave up raising silkworms?"

Henri shrugged his shoulders.

"I only meant that your grove is valuable," he explained kindly. "Do not forget that. Some time you might want money. I did not know whether you realized how much a big grove of full grown mulberry trees is worth."

"I never thought anything about it," was Pierre's thoughtful reply. "Our trees have never seemed to me anything I could sell. I thought only of gathering the leaves for our own use."

"Well, just remember that your silk-house and your trees are worth a good sum to a silk-grower. In these uncertain days of war one can never tell when money may be needed. Of course you might not be able to get such a good price for your property now, because France is poor, and everything is selling for less than usual—everything except food. Still, if you found the right customer you should be able to make a good many francs out of your homestead."

"It isn't mine," Pierre answered gaily, as if suddenly coming to himself. "It belongs half to my uncle and half to my father. What do you suppose they would say when they came back from the war if they found I had sold their mulberry grove and silk-house?"

"If you needed money for your mother and little sister they would probably feel you had done wisely, even though it caused them disappointment to see their cherished possessions in the hands of others. And if," added the elder boy gravely, "anything happened to them how glad they would be that those they loved were not left penniless."

"Anything happen to them!" Pierre's face paled. He had never, strangely enough, pictured such a calamity. *His father! His uncle!* True, other men were injured fighting for France, thousands of them. But surely no harm could come to *his* family. Those he loved would return when peace came; take up life where they had left it; and the home would once more be united.

The boy glanced up to find Henri studying his face sympathetically.

"I did not mean to make you sad, little brother," declared the elder lad softly. "The father and uncle will without doubt come again just as you say. But must we not all be brave enough to look at things squarely and with courage? Now that your father is gone to the war you have a man's work to do. Surely you are going to meet life like a man, not as a child. Forgive me if what I have said has hurt you."

With instant friendliness Pierre put out his hand.

"You have not hurt me," he returned quickly. "You have just set me to thinking. I'm afraid I have been pretty thoughtless. My mother must have had fears and have been worrying; yet so bravely has she kept it to herself that she has shown Marie and me only her joyous side. I might have helped her had I realized this before. She has always treated my sister and me as children, keeping from us everything that was hard. But I'll prove to her in future that I, at least, am no longer a child. Thanks to you, Henri, I will go home to Bellerivre not only wiser about silk-growing but wiser, I hope, about life."

"Perhaps, then, our talk has been fortunate," answered Henri, gazing earnestly into the upturned face. "I hope so. And maybe some time you will write to me and let me know how you are getting on. If I could ever help you about your silk-raising I'd be glad to. There might be something you'd like to ask. Henri St. Amant is my name, remember; and I am always here at Pont-de-Saint-Michel."

With a cordial clasp of the hand the two boys parted.

Little did Pierre know what a loyal friend his chance acquaintance of the morning was to prove.

CHAPTER X

THE AWAKENING OF THE CHRYSALIS

hen Pierre returned home he had much to tell his mother and Marie, you may be sure, of his visit to Pont-de-Saint-Michel, and of the new friend he had made at the Gaspard mills.

Now that the rush of handling the cocoons was over the days were not so crowded, and although there was still plenty to keep the Bretton family busy, Pierre and Marie resumed their normal routine of life, having daily lessons with Monsieur le Curé, and aiding their mother in the regular round of household tasks. There was a thorough cleaning of the silk-house that it might be in readiness for the coming season; then there was the money from the cocoons, the wonderful shining francs which the family had earned together, to be invested. Part of them were laid aside for living expenses; and part were spent in comforts for the loved ones who were in the fighting line.

As she now had more leisure Madame Bretton went each

day to the village church to work with the other women at stripping and rolling bandages; and when at home her deft fingers were never idle but flew to and fro at her knitting. Marie, too, had learned to knit and although she complained that her needles refused to *click* as did her mother's, she nevertheless was already able to make a sock and fashion its toe and heel without help. As for Pierre, he split the wood, cared for the cow and the goats, toiled in the field, brought hay from the hillsides, and assumed much of the heavy work which his father and uncle had been accustomed to do. A new manliness had crept into his bearing, causing his mother to regard him with puzzled surprise, and not a little satisfaction.

"You are a great comfort to me, Pierre," she would exclaim a score of times a day.

Once the lad had flushed with pleasure at overhearing her say to Monsieur le Curé:

"What should I do without my good son, my brave Pierre, to lean upon?"

Thus nearly two months sped past, and the moths within the cocoons that had been laid aside for breeding began to hatch out and force themselves through the small apertures they rent in their silken houses.

Marie viewed the first arrivals in consternation.

"They will fly all about the house and we shall lose them!" she cried. "What can we do with them?"

But Pierre only laughed.

"Have no fear, little sister," he answered reassuringly. "Josef says they will but flutter far enough to find their mates, and when their eggs are laid they will die."

"Alas," sighed the girl, "what a wee time they have to enjoy the glory of their new wings! Is it not sad, Mother?"

Madame Bretton regarded the child gravely for a moment; then she shook her head and smiled into her little daughter's troubled eyes.

"It is not so sad as it seems," she answered gently. "The silkworm has completed its work, and there is no need for it to live longer. It is so with all of us. Each is put into the world with a task to finish, and there can be no greater happiness than to know that that work—whatever it was—has been faithfully accomplished. To me the lesson of these tiny creatures' lives is an inspiration."

Marie smiled faintly, but was still unconvinced.

"But to have it all end just when they have got their wings, Mother!"

"But it does not end, chérie," was the quiet reply. "The moths leave behind them their eggs, which hatch into another family of silkworms. The work goes on, don't you see; it does not stop."

The girl's face brightened.

"It is so with children," continued her mother. "They live after their parents are gone, and carry forward the family name and the good principles their fathers and mothers have left in their keeping. You and Pierre will, I hope, take out into the world all the good things your father and I have attempted to teach you. Try to live always so that the name you bear shall be honored. We have been poor French peasants but we have never done anything that could cause you shame. And now in addition to that knowledge you will have it ever to remember that your father was a soldier of France, and when trouble came to our beloved land he gladly offered his life to serve her."

A light of exaltation glowed in the woman's eyes.

Pierre, who had stolen unnoticed into the room, thought he had never seen his mother so beautiful. There was something in her face that brought to his mind the Jeanne d'Arc statue in the village square.

Softly he bent and kissed her cheek.

With the gesture Madame Bretton seemed to rouse herself, and her grave mood instantly shifted into playfulness.

"Dear, dear!" she cried. "How serious we all are getting! It was your moths, Pierre, that set me moralizing this way. Our work with them is not yet done, either, for we must spread out the sheets of paper on which they are to lay their eggs. Then we can move the pairs of moths onto them."

She rose briskly.

"But how can we, Mother?" queried Marie. "When we touch them they will surely fly away, won't they?"

"No, dear. After the moths have found their mates they can be moved very easily. I have often seen your father take them gently by the wings and put as many couples as he could on large sheets of white paper. There they remained, and after their eggs were laid we removed the moths and folding the papers of eggs put them away for next season's hatching. The eggs were fastened so firmly to the paper that there was no danger of losing any of them. Now where shall we spread the papers for our own moths? They must be put well out of the sun and the strong light and also where there is nothing to disturb the butterflies—no mice or insects for example—or they will not lay eggs for us. Suppose we spread our papers

"GO ON TIPTOE"

in Uncle Jacques' room. It is not in use now and it is on the shady side of the house."

Rising, she crossed the floor and threw open the door of a vacant bedroom.

Pierre noticed a shade of sadness flit across her face.

"Uncle Jacques would be glad to think we are using his room, Mother," said the boy quickly. "He has always been so interested in the silkworms. Perhaps by the time the mulberry trees leaf again we shall have peace, and he and Father will be once more at home helping us hatch out these very eggs. Who knows?"

"Who knows indeed, dear? Only the good God who is watching over their lives! It may be as you say. The spring may see them back again. We must do our part to be ready for their coming."

From a drawer she brought out some large flat sheets of white paper and spread them upon table, bureau, bed, and chairs. As the room was long there was plenty of space.

"Now see how careful you can be in bringing in the moths. Go on tiptoe and move gently."

Slowly the pairs of greenish white butterflies were transferred to the papers. Scarcely one did more than flutter feebly.

"How long will it take before the eggs are laid, Mother?" inquired Pierre.

"From twenty-four to thirty-six hours—usually not longer than that. Each female moth will lay three or four hundred eggs."

"Shall we have room for so many?"

"Oh, yes," nodded Madame Bretton. "You recall how small they are—only about the size of the head of a pin."

"In the meantime what are we going to give the moths to eat?" asked Marie.

"Nothing. They are not hungry like silkworms. After they leave the cocoon they eat no food, and they will live but a few days after their eggs are laid. We must then gather up the sheets of eggs as quickly as we can, for if they are left exposed to the light and air they will hatch at once and then where should we be?"

"The entire crop would be lost!" gasped Pierre.

"Yes. Your father had a friend to whom that misfortune happened. He was careless and left the newly laid eggs too long in the light, and when he came back from the hills where he had gone on a few days' journey to cut hay the tiny silkworms were hatched and he had nothing on which to feed them. At that season the young mulberry leaves had gone by and, in fact, the trees were nearly bare. It was a good lesson to him; but it was a sad one, for the next spring he had to buy silkworm eggs, and they cost him many francs."

"We will be more careful than that, won't we, Mother?" Marie said.

"I certainly hope so, for we can ill afford to waste our money."

And the Bretton family were more careful. Within a day or two the great sheets of eggs were folded and put away in a dry, dark place where they would be safe until the spring when, as the children insisted, Father and Uncle Jacques might be at home again to share in the hatching and direct the raising of the new crop of silkworms.

CHAPTER XI

PIERRE TAKES ANOTHER JOURNEY

uring the next few weeks many a letter passed between Pierre and his new friend Henri St. Amant; and by and by came an invitation for Pierre to come again to Pont-de-Saint-Michel and spend the day visiting the Gaspard throwing mills, where the raw silk was twisted and prepared for weaving. The boy was all eagerness to go and his mother, too, favored the trip, for Pierre had been working very steadily and now had few pleasures. It seemed impossible to complete the never-ending round of duties, although with uncomplaining zeal Pierre kept patiently at them. Marie, it is true, helped with some of the lighter work; but she was not strong enough to do much outside the house. As for Josef, faithful as he was, the old man was aging rapidly and could do little more than potter about the place and direct things. Therefore the cutting of trees for fuel, the drawing of water, the building of fires all fell to Pierre's lot.

What wonder that with such constant use the boy's strength was daily increasing until he was becoming a veritable young giant? With no small satisfaction he beheld the muscles of his arms tighten and stand out; and when he swung his axe and brought down a sturdy sapling it was with a glow of pleasure that he heard it crash to the ground. Certainly there were compensations in hard work! Moreover was not every French boy who was too young to serve in the army being a man at home? He was but doing what all his friends were. Nevertheless the thought of a holiday did fill him with anticipation. To get into something beside his workaday clothes, and to mingle for an entire day amid new scenes, to say nothing of seeing Henri St. Amant again—what a delight it would be!

Madame Bretton caught a reflection from his happiness and that nothing should be left undone that should enhance the joy of her son's outing she broke over her rules of strict frugality and packed a luncheon for him, to which she added a few of the little luxuries which for a long time the family had denied themselves.

And so in high spirits Pierre set forth for Pont-de-Saint-Michel. How familiar every step of the journey seemed this time! And how good it was to find Henri St. Amant awaiting him in the office of the Gaspard mills!

"I have been working over time all the last week, so they are letting me have this morning to show you about the throwing mills," he explained, his eyes shining into Pierre's still brighter ones. "And at noontime when we have finished our round of the factory we can go down by the river, and while we eat our luncheon we can talk together. Therefore suppose we do not waste precious moments in visiting now, for we shall scarcely have time to see all I want to show you before the noon whistle blows."

Accordingly Pierre's box of lunch was stowed away in Henri's locker, and speeding across the little bridge that connected the filature with the throwing mills, the two boys entered the great factories.

"Before we go another step there is one question I must ask you," said Pierre, stopping in the doorway. "I want you to tell me why the twisting of raw silk into thread is called *throwing*."

"I'll try to explain it as well as I can, Pierre," answered Henri. "Maybe you have stuck me on the very first question you've asked," he added smiling. "All I know is that the operation of twisting, or throwsting, the fibres of raw silk has come to be abbreviated into throwing. The workmen are known as silk throwsters. It is an old trade. At the beginning of the sixteenth century there were throwing mills at Bologna which were so good that it is from them our present day machinery has been copied and perfected. Usually the work is done on commission—the manager, or throwster, receiving orders from weaving mills for exactly the sort of thread they wish to use."

"Isn't it all alike?"

"No, indeed! It varies in size according to the number of threads in a strand, and the number of twists and turns to the inch. Some materials that are to be woven require heavy, loosely twisted thread; others, that which is fine and tightly twisted. And in addition to these differences some thread is not made from pure silk, or even from silk of the best quality; raw silk which is imperfect can just as well be used for certain purposes, or silk that is twisted with a strand of cotton or some other filling. There are a great many qualities and kinds of thread and each one has to be specified."

Pierre opened his eyes.

"Organzine, for example, is used for the warp of woven silk materials and is generally spun from the best quality raw silk, the threads being firm and strong. Tram, on the other hand, is silk of a second grade and is composed of a greater number of fibres. Many of the mills manufacturing woven silks prefer not to own throwing mills. Often their plants are in large cities where land is expensive and they must economize space; or the manufacturers estimate that they can get thread thrown for them cheaper than they can do it themselves. Anyway, they either send their own raw silk here to be thrown according to certain specifications, or they tell us to get the raw silk ourselves and throw it into the varieties required. If the firm sends its own silk it comes to the throwster in bulk with an order to throw a certain proportion of it into organzine of so many threads and twists; and the rest into tram of specified size, the price being computed by the pound."

"I understand."

"The throwsting of silk is a great test of the reeling. If the reeling has been well done, and the size of the strand is uniform, we have no trouble; but if the reeling has been poor, and the gum not thoroughly soaked out of the filament, the threads will snarl and break when they are put on the machines. Frequently there is great loss from poorly reeled cocoons, as I think I told you. And you must keep in mind that the cocoon gives us two kinds of silk thread—the reeled silk, which is of the best quality and is the continuous filament wound from the cocoon requiring no textile machinery to prepare its fibres; and the spun silk, which is made from the loose floss taken off before the cocoon is reeled, or comes from cocoons that were too imperfect to be wound off by the reelers. The latter variety must be treated much as are the fibres from the cotton plant, or those of sheep's wool. By that I mean that the short lengths have to be twisted and spun together before they can be woven on a loom. Do you see the difference?"

Pierre nodded.

"Reeled silk comes direct from the cocoon, leaving the filatures on spools, as you saw when you were here before. After that it is brought to these mills and wound over into hanks or skeins of a specified length—usually from 333 to 500 yards. The foreman told me that long ago they had to employ one person to attend to every reel; but now with modern machinery a single girl can watch twenty-four spools at once. One of the interesting things is that all the finest reels used in France, Italy, China, and Japan, come from America."

"But why don't the Americans reel their own raw silk, then, instead of importing it?"

"They have no cocoons. My father says they tried raising silk in America, but it was not successful. Mulberry trees will grow in some parts of the country, but there is no cheap labor to be had over there as here, and therefore it costs too much to feed and care for the silkworms, and reel the raw silk. It is far less expensive for American merchants to import the reeled silk for their looms. But they can beat us at making machinery, if not at raising cocoons."

Henri chuckled.

"My father says," he went on, "that the Americans did not perfect the reeling machines so much for our good as for their own. They used to get all kinds of silk thread from the different parts of Europe; and it could not be woven on their looms, which are finely adjusted and require material of uniform size and strength. So they perfected machinery for the preparation of silk thread, and practically insisted that if they were to buy of us in Europe the material ordered must be made as they wanted it. Most of the countries over here were glad enough to comply with their demands, for the Americans are not only enormous buyers, but their machines are much better than ours."

"Why couldn't they have cocoons shipped to them in bulk?" speculated Pierre.

"They could not be easily packed, for they are not in form to ship. It would be foolish. Besides, there is the same old problem of the lack of cheap labor. You see, reeling silk is often slow work. Different breeds of silkworm turn out, as you know, different qualities of thread. You wouldn't believe how it varies as to size, cleanliness, lustre, and perfection of filament. The Americans cannot afford to pay people to classify all these varieties; nor stop their machinery at irregular intervals to pick out the imperfections, or slugs, as we call them; also the many knots must be tied by hand. It is fussy work. It would cost an American manufacturer lots of money to get the sort of thread he wants. You remember, too, how some of the best reelers that you saw when you were here before sometimes had to take as many as five or more filaments from different cocoons to get raw silk of a necessary coarseness; even then, in spite of all their care, the skeins have to be sorted and sometimes re-reeled to perfect the thread and make it acceptable to American buyers. Our weavers over here would not begin to be so particular; and in fact they often rate as *fair* stuff that the Americans consider *poor*, and refuse to take. You can readily see that all this preparation of the material can be done for less price in Europe, where workmen do not expect such high wages."

"What a lot of trouble the caterpillar makes people before his silk is ready for the loom!" exclaimed Pierre laughing.

"I guess you'll think so when you see all we have to do to it," agreed Henri. "I hope you won't mind the smell of the factory. It is horribly stifling, and makes some of the men sick at first. It is the oil and water in the silk. Silk must be damp for winding and spinning, otherwise it breaks. It is never, even at best, thoroughly dry, for it has the faculty of absorbing and holding moisture. Some time you'll learn more about how they have to allow for the moisture in silk when they weigh and ship it. Raw silk will often take up as much as thirty percent of its weight in moisture without any one suspecting it. Therefore, in order to be fair to the buyer who purchases his material by weight, they have in all great silk centres what they call silk-conditioning houses, where they test the goods to find out how much water is in it. This is done by an apparatus known as a *desiccator*, which tells what the silk would weigh if dry. To this estimate they add a definite percentage, ordinarily about eleven percent, to total what the raw silk would weigh with a normal percentage of moisture. Every purchaser must expect to pay for some moisture in his material—that is, pay more for it than the silk itself actually weighs."

Pierre regarded Henri mischievously.

"There seems to be so much to learn that I do not believe I shall get through this mill to-day. Maybe I'll have to spend the night here."

"I wish you could!" cried Henri. "Why didn't you plan to come home with me and stay until to-morrow?"

"I couldn't be away over night, Henri," answered Pierre, "although it is kind of you to ask me; there is so much that I have to do at home."

"Let us make haste then," Henri cried. "You have not seen anything yet, and the morning is passing."

CHAPTER XII

THE HOME-COMING

here are about a dozen different processes which taken together are known as throwing," explained Henri. "First the silk reeled from the cocoons must be wound; then cleaned of all gum; picked—which means that the uneven lumps must be removed; doubled, to make the thread stronger; twisted, to make it still firmer; rewound; and finally reeled all over again into silken yarn. Then it is ready to be put into any form desired, in accordance with orders received from the weaving companies. Sometimes it is made into what we call *singles*, one thread being given a twist to make it stronger. Sometimes, as I told you, it is made into *tram*, two or three threads being twisted lightly together just enough to hold them; tram, as I said, is used for the filling or woof of woven materials. Or perhaps *organzine*, which forms the warp threads of woven goods and is composed of two or as many more singles as desired, is ordered. Organzine can, of course, be made in any size specified, its coarseness or fineness varying with the strength necessary; and it can also be twisted any number of times to make it loose or tight. It must, however, be twisted in the opposite direction from the twist given it when the thread is made into singles or else that twist would come out and do no good. And just here is an amusing point and one that nettles the American buyers not a little. The moment raw silk is twisted even once, transforming it into singles, the custom-house officials on the other side of the water cease to regard it as a raw product although nothing in the way of actual manufacture has taken place in its preparation. The difference in its rating makes a difference in the duty levied on it. Odd, isn't it?"

"How do you come to know all these things, Henri?" demanded Pierre. "You seem to have studied everything there is to learn about silk."

"Indeed I haven't! But when you hear silk-making talked on every hand you can't help picking up more or less information about it. Let me be set down in a weaving mill, though, and I should be ignorant as a baby. The problems of weaving are not in my line. Here in Pont-de-Saint-Michel almost every one is employed in the Gaspard filature, or in the throwing mills; and if not, the people raise silkworms. Since the men have been called to the colors practically all the work of this big manufacturing plant is being done by women, boys, and children. The few men we have who are operating the heavier machines have either been sent home from the front because they were wounded or else they are not strong enough to fight. So you see, silk is the language of the whole village."

Henri gave a little shrug to his shoulders.

"It seems as if France must turn out enough silk for herself and all the world," observed Pierre, motioning to the great bales heaped in a near-by shipping-room.

"The output is, of course, very small now in comparison with what it usually is," answered the elder boy. "The war has made a great difference. Normally France does provide a good share of the world's silk. But other countries do as much, if not more. For a long time Asia sent most of the silk to the United States. Labor was very cheap in China, as well as Canton and Shanghai. The natives, however, employed very primitive methods in preparing their material and did it very poorly, often winding the raw silk on bamboo sticks that roughened or broke it. Frequently the thread would be a mass of dirt and slugs. Merchants would not stand for this, and now American manufacturers have gone to China and set up their own filatures equipped with American machinery."

"How stupid of China to lose a chance like that for trade!"

"The Chinese are the slowest of all the big nations to adopt new ideas, my father says; but they are waking up. They have been so clever in the past, and the foremost to discover so many things that it is a pity others should take from them the fruits of their learning. It is to China, people say, that we owe the entire silk industry. And careless preparation of their raw silk has not been their only or greatest crime."

For a moment Henri paused.

"No. About 1870 the Chinese silk dealers got it through their heads that what the American manufacturers demanded was a heavy silk thread. Now instead of selecting more carefully the cocoons from which they wound their raw silk and reeling it more perfectly, they set their ingenuity to work to increase the weight of the fibre itself by loading it with acetate of lead."

"I should think the Americans would have been pretty angry at that!"

"They were. They told the Chamber of Commerce at Shanghai that the United States would refuse to buy silk of China unless this practice was stopped. That scared the people, and for a while the adulteration of the material ceased. But the reform was not for long. From time to time the natives went back to their old tricks until by and by not only America, but even the greater part of Europe, got all out of patience with them. When they finally remedied the evil it was too late. Other countries had learned the art of silk-raising and had stepped in and snapped up most of the trade. My father says that now America, which is the largest silk consumer of the world, buys only about a quarter of her raw silk from China."

"So the evil-doer does not always prosper," laughed Pierre.

"Evidently not. In contrast to China's actions see what Japan did. That nation was enterprising enough to cultivate silk and foster its reeling; and when America sent the Japanese machinery they set it up and soon had tremendous filatures run by their own people. There were thousands of factories where whole Japanese families were employed in reeling silk from the cocoons. The Japanese raw silk, however, was not always free from gum, and in time there was so much complaint about this from America that conditioning houses were established at Yokohama where the goods of each merchant were examined and his personal trade-mark attached to his wares so if they did not come up to the standard they could be traced back to the owner who shipped them. Now more and more Japanese silk is sold, and in the main it is good, although America sometimes complains that it drops below the standard. Certainly no one can begrudge Japan her prosperity, since she had the wit to grasp her opportunity for commerce."

"Surely not."

"I think the trading of different nations one with another is all very interesting, anyway," went on Henri. "Why, we are like one big family—or ought to be! My father has no patience with war. He thinks we should try and overlook the other's faults as we do at home, and live together in peace. We all need each other, and the products peculiar to each land. No one of us can get on without the rest, for as yet no one country has been able to turn out everything its people require. It takes every climate and every national characteristic to bring together the produce of the globe. Besides, trade brings the different races closer together. One of the greatest pities of this war is its interference with commerce through which avenue we were all building up bonds of universal friendship and sympathy. It stands to reason that we understand the people of China or America better if we have dealings with them and meet them sometimes, than if we always stay here in France and read about them, doesn't it? And surely trade brings about greater prosperity everywhere."

"It was to bring back to France that prosperity and peace that your family and mine went to the war," murmured Pierre gently.

"Yes. And if this can be accomplished, and this frightful war be the last war of the world it will be worth all that we have sacrificed," returned the older boy fervently. "But peace is a long time in coming."

He sighed.

"And prosperity will be still longer, I fear," added Pierre soberly.

There was an instant of tense silence.

Both boys were thinking.

"Speaking of commerce," resumed Henri, breaking in upon the serious tenor of the moment and speaking in his former tone, "you doubtless know that before the opening of the Suez Canal, London was the great raw silk centre of the world; now our own Marseilles leads, or did before this fighting began. And we must not leave out Italy when talking of silk-growing nations, for our neighbors, the Italians, have done as much if not more silk exporting as has France. You see their climate is ideal for raising silkworms; and when they are not beset by a plague that destroys their crops, as it did between 1864 and 1878, the industry prospers wonderfully with them. The thread from the Italian cocoons seems to be naturally stronger than ours, and some of the best quality raw silk in the world comes from small Italian villages. Then, too, of course Italian labor is cheap. While in France we pay unskilled reeling operatives from twenty to twenty-five cents a day Italian workmen doing the same thing get only fifteen or twenty cents. There is not so much American machinery used in Italy as here, however, and therefore some merchants in the United States prefer French to Italian thread. But generally speaking the very finest and highest priced silks made in America are manufactured from French or Italian material. For many purposes where less perfect thread is required the Americans use silk from the East. It is cheaper, and manufacturers cannot afford the more costly Italian and French thread for everything they make. Importing the material in bulk, even compactly as it is shipped, is enormously expensive. For you see there is always the chance of loss in the silk business."

"Why?"

"Because although silk is necessary in the manufacture of certain indispensable articles it is for the most part a luxury, and the demand for it fluctuates. When times are hard people go without silk gowns and silk stockings; nor do they expend their money in silk, satin, brocade, or velvet hangings. The fashion, too, has much to do with the demand. Some seasons women wear only satins and that throws back on the manufacturers the silks they have on hand; or velvets are worn and the satins have to be shelved. The vogue of certain colors also often causes loss. It is a great lottery to be a silk merchant, my father says."

"Certainly the silkworm creates lots of business for people," declared Pierre smiling.

"And the thread for weaving sarsnet—or sateen, taffeta, satin, and velvet, as well as providing the fibres for sewing-silk is not all the little caterpillar gives, either. Had you thought of the oiled silk, used for a thousand and one purposes? Or of the silk-gut we use near the hooks of our fish-lines?"

"I fish with just a string," replied Pierre.

Henri chuckled.

"You are not an expert fisherman then, Pierre," he answered. "Still, one can land a very good fish with a pole and string; I have done it scores of times. But professional fishermen have a bit of silk-gut to connect the hook with the line. Not only is it very strong, but it is invisible when under water. Most of the silk-gut is made in Italy or Spain, the Spaniards surpassing all others at manufacturing it. Valencia is the chief centre for the industry."

"And how is it made? Spun from silk fibres?"

"Not at all. You remember how, before the silkworm begins to spin, the viscid secretion is stored in the two long ducts at each side of the little creature's body. It is that material which it unites into a single thread in the spinaret, you know. Well, before the worm has a chance to spin, it is put into vinegar and this jellied silk is extracted. It is first soaked in cold water and afterward in a caustic solution so that its outer covering can be loosened and taken off. Then the yellowish gum is dried in a shady place and bleached white by means of sulphur fumes. You can see that it is expensive because so many silkworms must be sacrificed, and because the thread produced is so small. Why, I have read that it takes as many as twenty or thirty thousand strings to make a pound."

Pierre gasped.

"No wonder I don't use silk-gut on my fish-line!" he exclaimed.

In the meantime the boys were passing on amid the stifling atmosphere and whirling machines.

Suddenly the noon whistle blew and the busy wheels of the mill became still.

Pierre and Henri were only too glad to emerge with the others from the close, steamy air of the factory into the coolness of the outdoor world. Down by the river's bank they

A ROYAL FEAST

unpacked their luncheon, a royal feast, for Madame Bretton had sent enough food for both hungry boys. They were in jubilant spirits.

"If I had a line with some silk-gut on it I might perhaps land a trout," said Pierre mischievously.

Henri shook his head.

"There are no fish in this stream, because the waste from the mill flows into it. But some day in the spring, when I have a holiday, I can show you a brook up in the hills where you can catch as many trout as you like—silk-gut or no silk-gut," he said.

"There are fishing-holes at Bellerivre, too," retorted Pierre proudly. "Why should you not make the next visit? You could then see my mother and my sister Marie; and I could show you our silk-house."

The sounding of the whistle cut short further conversation and warned the boys that their day together was at an end. Henri had to go back to the mill and resume work at his machine from which the kindly foreman had released him in the morning; and Pierre must take his train home.

But what a perfect day it had been!

As the engine hurried him toward Bellerivre Pierre busied himself thinking how much he would have to tell his mother and Marie. The village was reached almost before he realized it, and as he descended from the train he was surprised to find Monsieur le Curé standing on the platform to greet him.

The face of the priest was pale, and with apprehension Pierre made his way toward him.

"My son!" was all the old man could say.

Instantly Pierre knew.

"You have bad news, Father," he cried quickly. "It is from the war. Tell me! Do not fear. I am no longer a child."

Trembling, the kindly friend put a hand on the boy's shoulder.

"It came this morning—the message," he said. "I did not tell your mother, but waited for you. There has been another great battle and——"

"My father?"

"He is missing, Pierre."

"And Uncle Jacques?"

"He will come no more, my son. He has given his life for France."

CHAPTER XIII

PIERRE TAKES THE HELM

ilently Pierre received the news. He neither trembled nor cried out. In a vague way he realized that ever since that day long ago when Henri St. Amant had first presented this possibility to his mind he had unconsciously been bracing himself to meet with courage some such emergency. And now the blow had fallen, and it was he who must break the news to his mother, and be the strong prop on which she might lean. So busy was he with these thoughts that he scarcely sensed the presence of the faithful old priest who walked beside him. A score of confused reveries were surging over the boy, and out of the chaos of grief, reminiscence, and wonder, clearer ideas began to form themselves.

"We must sell the place," he declared, thinking aloud. "That will give us some ready money to start on."

"I, too, think that might be well."

It was the quiet voice of Monsieur le Curé.

"Forgive me, Father," said the lad. "I had forgotten——"

"Do not reproach yourself, my son," replied the priest gently. "I did not accompany you to be a burden in your sorrow—only that I might help if I could."

He laid his hand on the boy's shoulder.

Pierre glanced into his eyes gratefully.

"About the selling of the home—you think it would be wise?" he asked.

"It seems to me now to be the best plan; but I should wish to consider the matter more carefully before I gave a final decision. Advice must not be given too hastily."

"You see," continued Pierre, still formulating his ideas, "the constant care of a large crop of silkworms is too hard for my mother and Marie. We have been able to manage it one season, and we might even do it two; but to feel we must work as hard as that forever—it is not to be thought of. If we are to take up sericulture permanently we must have more help, and with the comparatively small margin of profit we are able to make we are not in a position to do that. When my father and uncle were at home it was a very different thing. Of course I have Josef, but he can do only the lightest part of the work. I am glad to do my share, more than my share; but I am only a boy, Father, and not so wise nor so strong as my father was. Nor have I his knowledge. If our crop of cocoons should fail some season either through my lack of skill or because of some unavoidable calamity, we should be without money on which to live. It would be terrible. The thought fills me with fear. Help me, Father. You are older than I. Give me your counsel. Do you think I am right, or only a coward?"

"To face the truth is never cowardly, Pierre," answered

the priest. "You reason well, my son. To take upon yourself in future the care you have borne this year is far too much for a lad. It is a work for several able-bodied men. That you and your mother and Marie have been able to do it even this once is little short of a miracle. Of course you have each thrown your entire heart and strength into it. Then, too, the season has been ideal. No calamities have befallen your crop. Nevertheless misfortunes do come. There are distempers that ravage the silkworms; bad weather that wrecks the mulberry foliage; a thousand possible accidents which at any moment may sweep away your income. Such a reverse would be a dire catastrophe to you and your family." The curé paused thoughtfully. "But if you were to sell the place," he went on a second later, "what would you do? Surely the sum you would receive for it, even if it was a generous one—a thing we can hardly expect in war time—would not be sufficient for you all to live upon."

"I should not try to live here," answered Pierre promptly. "Long ago I made up my mind that if anything befell my father and my uncle I would persuade my mother and Marie to go with me to America."

"America!"

"It is not so far away."

"It is at the other side of the world!" asserted the simple priest.

Pierre laughed.

"No, indeed, Father. America is but a ship's journey away. Besides we have relatives there. My mother's people are all at Paterson, New Jersey. My plan would be to take part of the money we get for our home and with it pay our passage to

America. There I could find work at good wages, and take care of my mother and sister."

Monsieur nodded silently.

"All this," continued Pierre, "is in case my father is not found. You tell me he is missing. What does that mean, Father?"

"It may mean any one of several things," returned the curé. "Your father may have been wounded and carried to some enemy's hospital; he may be a prisoner in some war camp; or——"

The old man faltered.

"Or——" persisted Pierre. "Speak, Father. Do not be afraid."

"Or he may have fallen, and be lying unclaimed on some distant battle-field."

"And what do you think is the chance of his being heard from?"

Unflinchingly the boy put the question.

"We cannot tell. He is in God's hands. I should wait for a time, my son. Then if no message comes we must——"

Again the kindly voice wavered.

"We shall know he has been lost," put in Pierre in a whisper.

"I fear so."

Stillness fell between the two. Each was thinking.

"Then for the present I will not speak yet to my mother of selling the home," said Pierre at last. "We will wait and hope for good news. It is cruel to distress her unless we must. All may yet be well. Surely she has grief enough as it is, for she was very fond of my uncle."

"You are a wise lad, Pierre," exclaimed the curé. "Do as

you have said. Console your mother with the hope of good tidings from the front. They may come—who knows? And if not, her sorrows will at least come singly and not all at once."

And thus it came about that through the great grief that overwhelmed the Bretton home it was Pierre who was his mother's stay and comfort. He it was who counseled hope and patience; he who took up the burden of acting both as father and son.

But despite his courage the message so eagerly longed for did not come. Days, weeks, months dragged on. The winter passed and faint hints of spring began to steal into the landscape. The river, foaming with the melted snows from far up the Pyrenees, dashed with deafening roar through the mountain gorges. There was a new brilliancy in the noonday sunshine.

To Pierre the worst had now become a certainty. His father would never again be heard from. Somewhere in a camp or battle-field far from home like a true son of France he had given up his life for his beloved country. With sinking heart the boy faced this reality. He had not sensed until now how subtly a secret anticipation that the facts might prove otherwise had buoyed him up. But now hope was gone. How should he tell his mother? How break in upon the dream she was cherishing, and rudely force upon her the need for action?

How would she receive the plan for selling the home? To leave the spot she loved so much would be an overpowering blow to her, for had she not come as a bride to her present dwelling? Nay, more; she had been born in Bellerivre and had never ventured beyond its confines. What would she say to breaking every tie of her old life and setting forth from the valley she loved to end her days in a strange and unknown country? For Marie and himself it was well enough; they were young and their days stretched far before them. But for his mother it would mean only the severing of every familiar association.

Poor Pierre! Many an anxious hour did he spend wondering how he was to present his plan so that it would not seem cruel.

Then one day he suddenly saw how useless had been his worry. It was his mother herself who spoke and made the very suggestion he had been hesitating to voice. How calmly and with what courage she did it! Ah, Pierre need not have feared that she would fail to meet the great issue when it came! Madame Bretton was too much of a woman for that. Instead she had a long talk with her children and afterward a letter was dispatched to the relatives in that mystic land, America. Soon a reply came back. Madame Bretton had come of fine peasant stock, and her brother had carried with him into the new land of which he had become a citizen his native loyalty and bigness of heart. He now wrote urging his sister and her fatherless children to come to Paterson and share his home until such time as they could find work and settle themselves in some convenient community.

And when this was agreed upon who should come forward to Pierre's aid but Henri St. Amant! He it was who found at Pont-de-Saint-Michel a customer ready to purchase for a good price the Bretton homestead, with its well-equipped silk-house, and its grove of thriving mulberry trees. Together with Pierre and the curé he worked out every detail of the Brettons' departure, acting with a wisdom that was amazing in so young a lad. The faithful Josef was to have a home with the old priest; nothing was forgotten. Certainly Henri was a friend in need!

Therefore one sunny morning the Brettons started south across France for the seaport from which, a week later, they were to set sail for that untried world toward which many another hapless exile had journeyed, and within whose borders the refuge of a home was offered.

CHAPTER XIV

PIERRE AS A TEACHER

It appalled Pierre to see how much of the little fortune received from the Bretton homestead had to be expended in reaching America. The money which had seemed such a fabulous sum in Bellerivre evaporated in the new land like the dew before the sun. Madame Bretton was too independent to consent to live with her brother's family and be a burden to them longer than was absolutely necessary, and therefore the renting and furnishing of a simple apartment became unavoidable. After this expenditure but a small bank account remained, and this the family agreed must not be cut in upon; something must be left in case of illness or disaster. In consequence the only way left to meet the expenses of daily living was for all three of them to take positions in the great silk mills, where so many hundreds of others were employed.

This was a great mortification to Pierre. Not that he was ashamed to have his family rated as working people. Every one in the world, at least those who were useful, worked in one way or another. His humiliation lay in the fact that he who had thought himself able to be the breadwinner for both mother and sister, was in reality nothing but an unskilled laborer, whose services for the present commanded but slight remuneration. The discovery was not only disconcerting but galling. It was bad enough to have Marie enter the mill. But his mother———! To think of his mother, at her age, becoming a mill operative!

If the step was as repugnant to Madame Bretton as to Pierre she at least made light of it. They must all live, she cheerily explained, and living in America was a far different problem from what it had been in the green valley of Bellerivre. And after all they were but doing what many another household in Paterson was doing. Why should it be any less dignified for her to labor in a mill than at raising silkworms? Besides, it might not be for long. When Marie and Pierre learned and became more expert maybe they would earn enough so that she could retire and stay within doors like a lady of fortune, keeping the home and— she jestingly added—dressing in some of the very silk she had helped to make. Thus with affectionate banter Pierre's objections were quieted if not overcome, and through the influence of Mr. Gautier, Madame Bretton's brother, who was a superintendent in one of the larger mills of the plant, good positions were found for the entire family.

Fortunately both Marie and Pierre were of an age to pass the Child Labor Laws of the State, an important detail of which Pierre had previously been in ignorance. Many children who applied for places, he learned, were constantly being turned away because they were too young; and because much of the work formerly done by them was now performed by women or girls.

Among the toilers in the vast manufactory almost every country was represented. There were more Italians than any other nationality; and ranking after them came Germans, Irish, and Dutch, with a scattering of French and Poles. It made the Brettons feel quite at home to find themselves among some of their own countrymen.

But what a different place Paterson was from the fertile valley they had left behind them! There were the great blackened factories—a city in themselves—with their tall chimneys and whirring wheels, which one came to hear almost in one's sleep. And there were the homes huddled closely together into which humanity was herded. Even the blue of the sky was dimmed by a veil of heavy smoke. What wonder that it took all the Brettons' courage to be cheerful under such conditions; or what marvel that many a time they sighed in secret for that far-away land where they had been born? But there must be no looking backward. Resolutely they crushed the homesickness that surged up within them, and began to learn all they could of this strange new country which in future was to be their home.

Paterson, their Uncle Adolph explained, had become the greatest silk centre of the United States, because it was so near New York, the city where most of the raw silk from European ports was received.

"But I do not understand why the factories are not built in New York itself," remarked Pierre.

"Taxes are too high and land is too expensive to afford the necessary area for such great mills as these," explained his uncle. "Small silk goods which can be made in little space are manufactured in New York; in fact, the headquarters for American laces, fringes, trimmings, and tassels is there. To have an ideal location factories must be so situated as to be near a large city which will assure the selling of goods, their shipment, and the chance to secure plenty of labor for the mills. Moreover, they must be built where, as I said, land is comparatively low priced and plentiful, and the taxes moderate. Such a combination is not easy to find. It explains why so many cities have in them the kinds of manufactures they have. It is an interesting study to follow out. Here in New Jersey, for example, we have throwing and spinning mills, large dyeing establishments, and we weave the finest of ribbons as well as broad goods."

"What do you mean by broad goods?"

"The term applies to dress materials and the silks that are sold in the shops by the yard," answered his uncle.

"Pennsylvania, too, is a large silk-making community," went on Mr. Gautier, "because fuel is cheap in that State; and because, since so many of the Polish, Irish, and German men work in the mines, silk mills afford a livelihood for the great numbers of unemployed women, girls, and young boys in their families. In fact the State of Pennsylvania often gives to companies that will come into the mining districts and put up silk mills not only the land for their factories, but also sites for the homes of their employees. That is one thing that has brought so many silk mills into Pennsylvania. Quantities of ribbons and broad silks are made there, as well as velvets and upholstery goods. It is a great throwing and spinning centre."

"Tell me something about the other States," demanded Pierre, his eyes wide open with interest.

"Well, there is Connecticut—that is a large silk-making district. About two-thirds of the machine twist is manufactured there; and they turn out both narrow and broad goods—silks, velvets, plushes. At South Manchester some of the finest and most artistic American silks are made. Massachusetts stands at the front in the manufacture of sewing-silks, which require finely equipped plants and much heavy machinery; embroidery silks, wash-silks, and trimmings are made there, too."

Mr. Gautier paused a moment.

"Then there is Rhode Island," he continued. "That is a silk manufacturing State also, although it does not turn out anywhere near so much material as do the others that I have mentioned. If you want to be in the largest silk-making spot in America Paterson is the right place," he added, smiling down at his nephew. "There is no end of chance for a bright boy to rise in these mills. But you must be quick and work hard. You seem to be able to do both those things, Pierre. Just go to it, my boy, and you need not fear but you will be earning good wages soon."

In spite of his French ancestry Monsieur Gautier had caught the American slang.

Pierre glanced up into his face.

"I shall do my best for my mother's sake, if for no other," he replied.

"Well, you'll certainly have your chance to work here," laughed his uncle. "There is variety enough to please you, too. We have throwing mills; a place where we dye silk in the skein; a winding and weaving plant; another plant for

"I SHALL DO MY BEST"

dyeing goods in the piece; and a big printing and finishing plant. If you do not find something to suit you by the time you have worked through all these it will be your own fault. Of course women have the monopoly of certain parts of the work; but there is plenty left to go 'round, so do not worry."

With a twinkle in his eye Monsieur Gautier went into his office.

During the weeks that followed many new experiences did the Bretton family have, and much did they learn of silk-making. From every source available they gleaned information, for being versed in silk-raising they were eager to know all they could of the rest of the process, especially Pierre. He found there were hand-looms for the making of finer varieties of silks which were manufactured in smaller quantities and were of individual design. On American power-looms, which were surprisingly light of construction and were handled with great ease, most of the other goods were made. It was remarkable that a machine costing comparatively little and so simple to operate should be so accurate in weave, and turn out so much work. As for the old Jacquard loom that in a former day had transformed the industrial world—it had been so altered and improved as to be hardly recognizable. Formerly, he learned, looms of Swiss and German manufacture had been employed in America; but these had speedily given place to the American high-power automatic loom, especially for the making of ribbons which were woven the same way as were broad goods, except that the shuttle was not a flying but a fixed one, that moved from side to side like a sewing-machine. So clever was the construction of these looms that they seemed to be little short of thinking creatures; when plain ribbon was to be turned out the operatives who were paid so much for the *cut* or ten yard piece, had little to do beyond seeing that there was plenty of thread on the spools, and that the ends were tied when broken.

For the more expensive and elaborate ribbons, however, more involved machinery was required. One device after another had been added to eliminate human labor, but even then these machines needed more persons to operate them. As a result of their complexity the speed of these intricate machines was less, and in consequence the price of making the goods was increased. Nevertheless there was a vast improvement over past conditions, when all overshot and embroidered effects had to be worked out on hand-looms. It enabled Americans to turn now to home manufacture for their ribbons. It was nevertheless true, Mr. Gautier explained, that much of the home market was created by the high tariff on the French ribbons still manufactured on hand-looms; these continued to be of choice design and of greater variety of pattern than were the American goods that had to be turned out in larger quantities on power-looms. Were it not that the American ribbons could be bought cheaper the French ones would probably, in many cases, be preferred.

About one half of the total silk output of America, Pierre was told, was in dress goods. Many of these were rich in quality, but many were not. The American women eagerly followed the fashions and were, as a class, far more concerned about having silk of a fashionable color than possessing that which would wear a long time. In fact, they did not wish materials to wear too long. Most of them were fairly well-to-do and were able to discard a garment when a passing fancy had been gratified, and after a thing was passé they would rather toss it aside than wear it out. In consequence shopkeepers, who studied the market as if it were a thermometer, refused to cumber their counters with expensive goods which must only be shelved after their color or design was out of date. Such conditions had created an American market for cheap silks such as was unknown in Europe where quality was a far greater factor in the sale of silk materials. In the United States these flimsy dress goods could be turned out with little expense on American power-looms by unskilled workmen, whereas in other countries experienced men were needed to make them.

As for the soft satins or messalines, they were made almost entirely in Europe because the cost of American labor was too great for them to be produced here. The operatives making them were paid by the piece and the process of weaving was a slow one. The heavy brocades and tapestries for upholstery were usually of such elaborate design and so interwoven with gold thread that to manufacture them on power-looms was practically impossible; and as hand-looms were required European hand-loom work was cheaper than American.

"The flaw in our power-loom is that double threads cannot be handled," explained Mr. Gautier to Pierre. "Any goods requiring such treatment must of necessity be made on hand-looms."

So little by little Pierre's knowledge grew.

Military and upholstery trimmings, he ascertained, could be turned out in large quantities on power-looms; but dress and cloak trimmings, which were more elaborate, were made in America only in comparatively small quantities and again because of their intricate patterns and gold threads Europe could produce them cheaper on hand-looms. If, however, the pattern desired was sufficiently simple, and a large enough quantity of it was ordered to make it pay the manufacturer to bother with setting it up it could be made on the American power-loom. Fancy braids were made chiefly in Europe from the floss or spun silk taken from the outside of the cocoon; but plain braids, Pierre was interested to know, were made in America as cheaply and well as in Europe, most of them being manufactured from artificial silk.

It was a great surprise to Pierre to find there was such a thing as artificial silk.

"I knew there were artificial flowers and artificial—well, almost everything," laughed Pierre to his mother. "But artificial silk!"

He gasped.

"What is it made of, Pierre?" questioned Madame Bretton, who had come to regard with wonder the fund of information her big son was acquiring.

"The man who told me about it said that cotton and the pulp from soft wood were used for one sort," he answered. "Another kind comes from dissolving cellulose in chemicals, and forcing this mixture through long tubes into some sort of a bath that makes the material come out in threads; these threads can then be wound, spun, washed, soaked, and dyed. Here in America most of the artificial silk which, by the way, is known as viscose, has cellulose in some form as its base, afterward being treated with different combinations of chemicals."

"What shall we do with you, Pierre, if you learn so much?" questioned Madame Bretton mischievously.

Pierre smiled.

"I'm going to learn every bit I can, so that I may soon work up to earning lots of money," he said. "Then you and Marie can leave the mills, and I can take care of you."

"You are a good son," his mother answered with an odd little catch in her voice. "But do not be distressed because we are in the mills. Indeed we are very happy there."

"You would make the best of anything you had to do, Mother; you're that sort," replied the boy, taking her hand in his. "But I know well it is hard for you to work at a machine all day when you have never been accustomed to it, and I do not mean you shall do it one moment longer than I can help."

"There, there, son——" his mother's eyes filled, and to change the subject she said briskly:

"And these artificial silks of which you were telling me— are they good for anything else but for making braids?"

"Yes, indeed. Nitro and viscose silks are more brilliant and lustrous than are real silks. They have no such soft feeling, however. They feel more like the harsh, loaded silks made from thread which has been chemically weighted. But they are coming into demand more and more for such purposes as the warp and filling of various sorts of fabrics, rugs, silk stockings, and upholstery materials. Here in this country, where electricity is in general use, artificial silk is a blessing, for it serves as a substitute in the insulating of electric light wires, and the manufacture of mantles for lights."

"How clever people were to find anything that could be used instead of the real, carefully nurtured cocoon silk," mused his mother.

"I know it. I suppose chemists worked at the problem a

long time before they solved it. That is the way most of the great discoveries were made. Still, the wild silk made by the moths of India is not carefully grown. From it the Oriental Tussah silk is made; then there is Eria silk, also an uncultivated product from India; the Fagara silk from China; and the Yamamai silk from Japan, which is next to domestic silk in value. All these are manufactured from silk spun by silkworms that have had no care. The foreman was telling me about it the other day."

There was a pause.

"What did you mean, Pierre, when you spoke of loaded silk?" questioned his mother. "I have heard the term used many times, but I have never understood it."

Pierre looked at her with amusement.

"Anybody would think that I was your schoolteacher, Mother mine!" he returned. "I feel very silly telling you things when you are so much older and wiser than I."

"I certainly am older; and I used to be a little wiser," replied his mother humorously, "but I shall not be so long. You see, dear, I never had much education and I am now too old to learn. But you are accumulating knowledge every day. You are like a sponge, Pierre. You seem to soak up every bit of information that you hear."

"I must get my schooling this way, Mother, since I can secure it in no other," answered the boy soberly. "And perhaps it is a good way after all, for since I am eager to know something I try and remember every scrap I hear. I may want to use it later."

"Your father used to say that no knowledge comes amiss," was his mother's soft answer. "How proud your father would be of you, Pierre!"

"But I must know more, and more, and still more, Mother, before I can get to the top!" exclaimed the boy eagerly. "And now to tell you of weighted silks. You see, in dyeing silk the material shrinks and loses about a quarter of its weight. Manufacturers found that by adding chemicals, or sugar and glucose during the boiling off, they could make up for this loss. That is how the custom started. Black silks, which shrunk the most, were treated first. Later the practice spread to colored, and even to white silks. Now, alas, the evil seems to have come to stay. Salts of tin in varying degrees are used in the dyeing of most silks, and the result is that the material becomes crisp and harsh so that it cracks when folded, and does not wear long."

"What a pity!"

"Yes. And yet perhaps the Americans, who are none too anxious to wear out their old clothes, are quite as well satisfied," chuckled Pierre.

"In what an endless number of ways silk is used!" reflected Madame Bretton.

"Yes. And when you have done with the ribbons, and trimmings, and braids, and silks, and upholstery brocades, and satins, think of the velvets and plushes that can now be made in this country in all sorts of fancy designs on power-looms instead of on hand-looms as formerly. Of course it is still cheaper to import certain kinds of velvets and plushes; but a great many of them are made here, as are the larger proportion of the velvet ribbons which are easily turned out on high-power machines."

"What about silk hosiery and underwear?" questioned his mother, much interested.

"Silk stockings and silk gloves, Uncle Adolph says, are a big American product. There is little finishing to them except putting the buttons on the gloves. In fact I read the other day that the silk used for them was only slightly adulterated, and that they were made even better than in Europe. But making underwear seems to be another story. Each garment manufactured has to be shaped as it is made, and therefore the process is a special one and the knitting is slow. This results in expensive labor, and a very limited output. After the seams are finished, the buttons on, the fancy braid and facings in place, and the final trimmings stitched where they belong, the profit is small. All this can be done much cheaper in Europe, and were it not for the protection of a high tariff, Uncle Adolph says, Americans would buy all such goods abroad. The tariff protects the American silk industry at every turn. I don't know where the United States would be without it! Then you must remember that after this silk underwear is done it is not sold to individual customers in any considerable quantity. Instead it retails piece by piece, and therefore every piece has to be folded and packed separately. No wonder such things are expensive here!"

"I never realized before how interesting the problems of making things were," said Madame Bretton, glancing up at Pierre.

"It is all fascinating when you take it as a whole. But if you just do one part of the work over and over and never connect it with the entire process, it is tiresome enough. Every workman should consider himself a link in the big chain, and try to make himself familiar with the other links. Then he will feel as if he is really doing something, and not just pegging away day after day as if he were a machine. That is why I want to learn all I can about silk as a complete industry. It makes winding bobbins and reeling thread a more important matter. Some firms, Uncle Adolph says, have moving picture lectures and by means of them explain to their employees the entire process of their particular industry so they will be more intelligent about what they are doing. I think that is a fine thing. Nobody likes to do some uninteresting thing over and over, week after week and year after year, unless he understands what he is doing. Even the money you earn doesn't help to make your work less monotonous. How can employers expect their men to have any ambition, or any desire to turn out flawless products unless they realize that each detail of a process makes the perfect whole? I mean to know every step of the road I am traveling so when I get to the top——"

"So when you get to the top you can make silk all by yourself," interrupted his mother, completing the sentence with a smile.

"Well, I'm going to know how, anyway," nodded Pierre. "And I wish to learn not only of silks and velvets, but laces, too. Laces are fussy, difficult, and expensive to make. I want to find out all about them. I know they have to have the strongest and most perfect thread. In Europe such goods are made either by hand, or on hand-looms. It is a slow process at best. But the power machines here, slowly as they are forced to work, can of course turn out lace much faster than it can be made in Europe on hand-looms. Consequently the commoner kinds of laces are made in this country, used, and worn out while they are in fashion; for the Americans shift their fashions in laces quite as fast as they do their fashions in silks. Before a certain design can be sent to Europe, manufactured, and sent back again the vogue for that particular pattern will have ceased and Americans will be wearing something else. That is what saves the lace trade for America. It is the same with the making of lace veils."

"There seems to be no keeping up with these Americans," laughed Madame Bretton. "Certainly there is no keeping up with their cost of living!"

CHAPTER XV

THE GREAT SURPRISE

uring the next few months the Bretton family prospered in their careers in the Paterson mills. Madame Bretton, whose deftness and care in handling material was quickly recognized, was promoted to a position much better suited to her age and refinement, and also one that was more lucrative. In addition Marie, skilful too of touch, was put in the labeling department. But with undaunted spirit Pierre still drudged at the heavier work of the mill, mastering one step after another of its dull processes. To another boy the slow climb to the top of the ladder might have been tedious; but to the French lad, with eyes fixed constantly on the great industry of silk-making as a whole, every part in the ingenious art became interesting.

Despite the fact that Mr. Gautier was his uncle the boy received no favors. In such a vast group of factories one superintendent had small jurisdiction over individual workers; nor was Mr. Gautier a man to promote unjustly. Whatever progress Pierre made he made on his own merits. On entering the mills he had been employed at *lacing*, one of the simpler tasks usually given to beginners. His duty was to run short threads in and out through the skeins of silk in order to divide them into four parts, and prevent them from becoming tangled in the dyeing. Many young boys and girls known as *lacers* were set at this task for the first month or two. But Pierre did not remain a lacer. He went on to being a learner in other departments.

He saw how the raw silk which arrived at the factories in bales ranging from eighty to a hundred twisted skeins were weighed; sorted as to quality; soaked in oil so that the gum might be extracted, and the ends freed for winding. He witnessed the drying, or rather the partial drying, of the silk. All this was an old story, for he had seen every step of the process before when at the Gaspard throwing mills. Then followed the winding on big, three-inch spools; and the first spinning. Afterward if the thread was for tram it went direct to the doublers, to be made stronger; but if it was for organzine it was spun again after leaving the doubling frames, and was given a much tighter twisting. It was then reeled into skeins again, this form being found the most convenient one for dyeing. The tying, or lacing of these skeins, had been Pierre's work. The skeins after being laced were then bundled, or packed tightly, to be sent to the dye-house. This finished the work of the throwing mills and Pierre was interested to see that the process was practically the same in America as in France.

But from the time the dyed silk came back to the weaving mills everything was new. The weaving of broad goods such as dress materials, mufflers, handkerchiefs, and necktie silks took place on the broad looms; while narrow goods such as ribbons were woven on the narrow looms. It was a long time, alas, ere Pierre came to understand the complex weaving machinery; and before he half comprehended it a most unexpected happening befell the Bretton family.

It was heralded by a letter from far-away Bellerivre—a letter from Monsieur le Curé; and before the amazing tidings in the missive could be assimilated another letter—a feeble scrawl—followed.

Monsieur Bretton lived!

The beloved father they had given up as lost was actually alive!

He had been wounded, captured, and kept a prisoner in a hostile camp from which it was impossible to communicate with his family. As soon as he was able he had been forced to work for his captors, and there he had remained cut off from all knowledge of his family or friends. By and by he had succeeded in escaping and reaching his own lines, only to be shot down in the next battle in which he had taken part. Then had followed a long illness in a French hospital where under the care of the kind sisters he had hovered 'twixt life and death. There had been no letters home because he had been too delirious to tell his nurses where to write. At length out of the chaos had come sanity, and now because his wounds were such that he could do no more fighting he had come home to Bellerivre. Monsieur le Curé and Josef were nursing him, and he hoped to join his dear ones in their new home as soon as he was able.

It was a wonderful story!

Some day, the doctor said, he would regain his strength

and be well enough to do some simple work so that he could still earn a livelihood and not be a burden to his family.

How good the tidings were! How almost unbelievable!

Over and over again the jubilant Brettons rehearsed the tale and framed new plans for the future. It took all Madame Bretton's resistance not to draw from the bank the treasured nest-egg still reposing there and go home to France to nurse her husband back to life. But Monsieur le Curé bade her not to come. The invalid was in good hands and progressing rapidly. Soon she might send money for the journey, and the kind priest himself would see the wounded Frenchman aboard a ship that would carry him to America. It was the wisest plan. Both he and Monsieur Bretton thought so. Then when peace was restored to the weary world, and the family had sufficient money they might all come back together to Bellerivre, never again to leave its sunny valley.

Thus argued the old priest.

But that day never came.

Pierre rose to a fine position at Paterson, enabling him to establish a pretty home there in which his father and mother lived in comfort. Marie, in the meantime, married an American and settled next door.

Thus the new land, once but a haven to a tempest-tossed household, became the permanent dwelling place of the Bretton family. Affectionately they remembered the green valley of Bellerivre; and the friendship of the old priest and the faithful Josef. Tenderly they spoke of their neighbors in the old home and ever loyally they loved La Belle France, the soil that had given them birth.

But the spell of America was upon them. They did not wish to go back.

The golden path of opportunity lay in the country of their adoption and in exchange for all that it was giving them they resolved to return a devoted citizenship.

And so between the two great sister Republics another bond was established—a humble bond to be sure, but one that linked in loving ties the old world and the new; and daily spanned the distance between them with many a kindly thought, and a speeding message of good-will.